CW01648234

Provoking Lord Simmons

WENDY MAY ANDREWS

Sparrow Ink
www.sparrowink.com

Copyright © 2022 Wendy May Andrews

All rights reserved. This book or any portion thereof may not be reproduced, transmitted, or used in any manner whatsoever without the express written permission of the author except for the use of brief quotations in a book review.

This is a work of fiction. Names, characters, places, and incidents are a product of the author's imagination. Any resemblance to actual persons, events, or locales is entirely coincidental.

ISBN - 978-1-989634-59-2

www.wendymayandrews.com

Stay in touch with Wendy May Andrews
and all her upcoming publishing news.

Sign up for her biweekly newsletter

She's the *opposite* of what he needs. Too bad she's all he wants...

Viscount Simmons, Lord Robert Scranton, knows he'll eventually marry. But that doesn't mean he'll choose the bride everyone keeps telling him he should. *Especially* when she might be a lovely (and entirely too tempting) enemy agent sent to thwart his case for the Home Office...

Isabelle Benedict wasn't trying to *thwart* anything. She was just researching potential husbands. The fact that her options *happen* to include a man Robert wants to investigate is irrelevant. What *is* relevant, however, is how attached she's quickly becoming to Robert...and how unlikely it is that he'll ever let her love him...

With his work, family drama, multiple misunderstandings, and past betrayals between them, Robert and Isabelle's path to happily ever after will *not* be easy. Fortunately, they aren't likely to give up without a fight...

***Provoking Lord Simmons*, the next book in the Northcott Kinship series is a lightly angsty, sweet and clean regency historical read featuring an opposites-attract, enemies-to-lovers, forced proximity romance. Download today and get ready to fall in love with Robert and Isabelle.**

Dedication

In *Provoking Lord Simmons*, Isabelle just wants a comfortable future, not necessarily glamorous or particularly special, she just wants to feel “at home” in her life. But sometimes that feels like a big ask. If you’re in that boat, here’s wishing for a place that feels like home for everyone.

XO

Acknowledgements

Acknowledgment number one has to go to my best friend and life partner, Mr. Andrews. Thank you for putting up with the late nights and stress snacking while I whittled away at this story. Thank you too for knowing and caring about my Northcotts nearly as much as I do. You're the best walking and talking partner a gal could ask for. Thanks for helping get in both my steps and my words.

Acknowledgment number two must go to my parents. Thank you for always standing by me and supporting me in all my endeavors. Thanks too for reading to me as a small child. I blame you for my love of words. It's still Aunt Marlene's fault that I adore the Regency era.

To my beta readers – Alfred, Monique, Suzanne, and Christina – thank you so much for cheering for me, finding the plot holes, and making such fabulous suggestions to help the stories improve.

My gorgeous cover is thanks to the artistry of Envision Literary Photography and Les at GermanCreative. I'm thrilled with my beautiful covers in this series.

Thanks to Kathleen Bosman for the great edits. Any remaining mistakes are entirely the fault of the author.

Chapter One

Lady Isabelle Benedict stared out the window of the carriage, bored and irritated, as her mother droned on about her failures. On the drive to Everleigh, the carriage had seemed well sprung and rather luxurious. Now, she would rather walk than remain inside any longer.

"Even that fast woman, Lady Constance, became betrothed at the house party. You should have tried harder. That should have been you. I don't know where we've failed with you, Isabelle. You are a disappointment, to say the least. Your sisters all managed to snare a husband in the first weeks of their debuts."

Isabelle didn't even bother to turn her head at this. She had heard it all before. The sad truth was that she wasn't even terribly disappointed in herself. While she would dearly love to get out from under her mother's despotic thumb, she had just barely turned eighteen the week of her debut and didn't feel that she was anywhere near to being on the shelf. It wasn't as though they were nearing the poorhouse. Isabelle couldn't quite fathom why her parents were so desperate to have her out of the house. It wasn't really going to change their lifestyle much, even if she were to need another Season. Since her father was an earl, he would be going up to Town to take his Seat in the House so it wasn't as though her mother wasn't going to be socializing.

Isabelle sighed. She supposed there were many more activities required if one was actively participating in the Season, particularly with an unwed daughter in tow. An unwed daughter who needed to be supervised at every single one of said activities.

"Perhaps we could have one of them accompany us to Town so the burden of escorting me doesn't fall solely upon you. I'm sure either of my sisters would be happy to do so," Isabelle thought to suggest as a help to her mother.

"And be accused of shirking my duty toward my failed daughter? I think not," Lady Bathurst scoffed.

Long gone were the sweet, dulcet tones Isabelle's mother had been using when speaking with her dear childhood friend, Lady Alcott, at the house party. Isabelle had marvelled over that relationship whenever she'd witnessed the two older women together. It hadn't seemed to strike Miss Alcott as odd, but it certainly had done so to Lady Isabelle. She had never seen her mother so girlish and relaxed. One could almost claim Lady Bathurst had been having a good time.

Those good times were clearly over now that she was enclosed in a moving carriage with her last unwed daughter.

Isabelle wondered if she ought to try to inquire about her mother's determination to marry her off but wasn't sure how to do so. Lady Bathurst had never been the most open of mothers, nor had she been affectionate or one to share her feelings. Isabelle didn't know how to ask something that felt personal in the moment.

"Father, is all well upon the estate?" she finally asked when her mother's current diatribe had finally droned to a conclusion. Isabelle might not be able to get the information she wanted from her mother, but there might be another way. Perhaps they were in need of marriage settlements or some such, after all, and just hadn't bothered to give her that detail.

"Yes, all is well, my darling daughter," Lord Bathurst replied promptly with a sideways glance at his wife. "Why do you ask? You know I haven't been there since we've been in Town."

"No, of course not, but surely Stanley writes to you."

"The estate is in good hands with him. I don't need to hear from him overmuch."

That was not getting her the information she sought. Isabelle stifled a sigh and returned her gaze to the passing scenery. It wasn't very inspiring even though it was lovely. Sitting in the rear-facing seat and staring out the window was going to turn her stomach if she wasn't careful. She would dearly love to pull out a book and while away the time, but her mother was sure to object.

'If you weren't such a blue-stocking, you'd surely be wed by now,' was one of her mother's favorite complaints even though she had only made her debut six weeks prior.

Isabelle wasn't certain if she even wished to wed. Well, of course, she did, she corrected herself. She just didn't want to pursue it in such an urgent manner. It caused her more anxiety than it ought to. Shouldn't such an important decision be made after much deliberation and consideration? She wouldn't have thought it ought to be rushed into with the first gentleman who showed the least bit of interest. Just his noticing her didn't strike Isabelle as the primary qualification she ought to be looking for in her future lord.

"You should have tried harder."

Isabelle tried not to sigh audibly. She had thought her mother was finished ranting at her over her so-called failings at the house party. Apparently not.

"That handsome viscount, Lord Simmons, would have been a good match for you."

"What makes you say so?" Isabelle decided that rather than argue or rail against her, she might as well try to understand her mother's reasoning.

"He seemed kind. And it is rumored he has ten thousand pounds a year."

Isabelle blinked. That *was* a goodly sum. But surely being wealthy wasn't the only consideration she ought to take. Nearly every one of their acquaintance had a measure of wealth.

"What made you think him kind?"

This question stopped her mother in her tracks, it seemed to Isabelle, and the older woman had to think on her answer for a moment.

"I never heard him raise his voice, for one thing," Lady Bathurst began, and Isabelle almost laughed out loud which would have been disastrous. Minding her tongue encouraged her mother to continue. "Everyone speaks well of him," was the next evidence the countess presented.

"You were always so high in the instep from what I remember of my sisters' debuts. Why are you now pushing me toward a viscount when you wanted my sisters to wed no lower than an earl?" It wasn't a matter of great importance to Isabelle, but she wondered why her mother had changed so drastically when it came to her youngest child.

"There aren't that many dukes lying about the *ton* anymore, Isabelle, and you needn't be such a stickler. It would be better for you to have success in the Marriage Mart, wouldn't you think?"

Finally, Belle couldn't help it; she had to laugh. "I wasn't the one thinking I ought to wed so high, Mother. I was asking about your about face on the subject."

Her mother merely sniffed and ignored the question. "You need to wed, Isabelle; surely, you realise that."

"I will eventually, but I see no need to rush into a decision that I will have to live with for the rest of my days."

"Have you not been thinking about this decision for *all* of your days?" Lady Bathurst demanded.

"Not really," Belle countered. "I was a child up until only very recently," she pointed out. "Marriage with anyone other than a fairy-tale prince didn't even cross my mind except in the most abstract of ways."

"Well, it's time for you to get on with it. Your father and I are ready."

Belle laughed again. "I'm glad for you, but has it occurred to you that I might not yet be ready?"

"You should have thought of that before you made your debut," Lady Bathurst countered with a caustic tone.

"I am again left to wonder why the urgency, Mother. While both my sisters did wed in their first Season, I don't remember them having been hurried into it. I don't understand why I cannot wait another year or two."

"Do you really wish to sit upon the shelf?" Lady Bathurst demanded.

"It's hardly sitting on the shelf when I'm only eighteen, Mother. And waiting for another Season is hardly an unprecedented delay."

"That may be, but I have no wish to dally."

Belle sighed and turned her attention back to the passing scenery, allowing her mind to drift back toward the house party they had just left.

Her mother wasn't wrong. Lord Simmons had seemed lovely in certain ways. But Belle couldn't find it within herself to set her cap at anyone, especially not a gentleman who seemed exceedingly aware of his eligibility. Somehow, despite her innocence, it struck Belle that it would be the worst situation to find herself in if a gentleman thought he had settled for her.

She wasn't deeply romantic nor so unrealistic as to expect a deeply abiding love match such as it would seem were arranged at the Everleigh house party they were driving home from. Belle had received the impression that all three betrothed couples were deeply enamoured with each other. She had been completely charmed by the various relationships she had witnessed. They had been so varied. The paid companion becoming engaged to Lord Merton had been a surprise, but then they had all found out that it had been a long-standing affection. Then there was Mr. Northcott and Miss Alcott who had grown up as neighbours. They had been friends as children, and then some sort of disagreement had led to an estrangement for years. But they had come together at the house party in such a romantic way. If one was inclined to romanticism, of course, which Belle was not, she reminded herself.

Lady Constance and Miss Alcott's brother falling in love had been, perhaps, the biggest surprise. The blue-stocking eccentric who travelled the world hadn't seemed a likely match for the gentleman who never left his estate, but it had been evident to anyone who looked upon them that their devotion was deep. It had been both entrancing and disconcerting, making Belle wonder what was wrong with her that she did not long for such devotion herself.

But there had been something about that viscount, Lord Simmons, that had caught her eye when she'd first arrived in Town. He was a pleasure to look at. Not quite so flashy as say, Viscount Adelaide whose wife hosted the house party, nor as large and brawny as Mr. Alcott, one of the newly betrothed, but his handsome features certainly drew the eye. And even though he appeared just as fashion conscious as the rest of the gentlemen of the *ton*, Belle hadn't been able to avoid noticing, the couple of times they had danced together, his hands weren't nearly so delicate as most other gentlemen which led her to believe that he was a man of action, and that was something to take note of.

Despite her resistance to her mother's determination to marry her off with the greatest of haste, Isabelle had every intention of marrying one day in the not-too-distant future. And there, she couldn't help finding a man of action to be of the utmost appeal. Perhaps it was because she feared her father was a lazy lout. Or because her first love as a young girl was the hard-working groom who had taught her to ride. But Isabelle had always had a soft spot for men who could work hard at manual labour which ruled out most of the gentlemen of the *ton* from what she could tell.

Not to say Lord Simmons didn't fit right in with the other gentlemen of the *ton*, she mused. He was so fashionable, one could almost consider him a dandy or a fop. Almost but not quite. Belle wasn't sure if it was the way he held himself or something in his eyes, but there was definitely a quality about the man that set him apart from the true fops and fribbles. Lord Simmons might dress the part, but he didn't quite pull it off. *In the best of ways,* her mind insisted even as she tried to reject the ideas being planted by her mother.

Despite her attraction to the viscount, there was something about him that held her off. She had no desire or intention of doing something so ill advised as to set her cap at him, that was for certain. Not that she would set it at anyone, for that matter. The very idea curdled her stomach and struck Belle as being the least dignified thing a woman could do, despite the fact that it seemed quite common amongst the ladies making their debut. Common was not a moniker to which Belle aspired.

She was determined that if nothing else, her husband would respect her. And how could he do so if she were to throw herself at him? Surely, if she were to be too easily won, she would be no prize for a man. Having brothers had taught her that, if nothing else.

Surely, no man wished to be chased. At least not the sort of man she could consider to wed. It was most odd that Lady Bathurst wasn't more aware or understanding of that.

In fact, Isabelle knew that her mother was very well aware of that. She could almost hear the woman, in her mind's eye, telling her sisters that very thing when they were making their debuts.

'Don't seem too eager or they'll think you easy. No man wants an easily won prize.'

And yet here she was urging Isabelle to do just that. It hadn't been such a long time since her sister closest in age had debuted, that the ways and standards of the *ton* had changed that drastically. And human nature surely hadn't changed.

Nerves clenched Isabelle's midsection. Perhaps it was as she thought: her parents' estate must be foundering, and they were counting on her to solve the matter in the time-attested way.

But surely they ought to be a little more open with her on the matter, Belle thought with exasperation. If they were, she might have handled things differently. As it was, she had been in no rush. In fact, she had been resistant to any gentleman's advances out of an ennui toward marriage. If she had been told her family needed her to wed, she would have taken the matter far more seriously.

But then, when she considered that no expense had been spared on her gowns and all the other accruements that went along with a debut, she couldn't imagine that they were short of funds. Surely, there would have been ways to economize had they needed to.

While Belle was well aware that appearances were vital, since all the debutantes had to dress similarly, it really wouldn't have mattered much if she had frequented a less expensive modiste, surely. She had never tried to do it, of course, but she was reasonably certain that economizing wouldn't be so challenging when one considered how very wasteful the entire Benedict family had always been.

Further reflection led her to understand, though, that it was likely that very wastefulness that would make the task of economizing a challenge for the family. If they had never done it, it would likely be a difficult thing to learn. But she, for one, would much rather do that than be rushed into marriage with whichever rich gentleman offered first.

But perhaps the rest of her family would rather she be sacrificed than to change their ways. What a lowering thought. Belle fought the surge of heat that prickled behind her eyes. It would not do to burst into tears in the carriage. That was certain to have her clapped up in bed with a tisane at the very least. At worst, she'd be recommended for Bedlam. Considering how oddly her parents were behaving, she wasn't certain which way they'd decide, and she wasn't willing to risk it.

Belle's midsection clenched. It was not the least bit comforting to think that she couldn't react naturally nor ask reasonable questions of her parents. Where had they gone so wrong? Had it always been thusly and she'd just been too youthful to notice? Or had something changed in recent times?

She was inclined to think something must have changed since she was nearly absolutely certain things had been different for her sisters. She ought to write to them and ask.

Belle began to compose the letter in her mind as a way to while the hours of tedium:

Dear Florence:

Mother and Father seem to have lost their minds and wish me out of the house at the soonest possibility. Send help.

That letter would get her in trouble for certain, but it helped to chase away the threat of tears.

Dearest Florence,

I trust you and your family are well. I am not having the level of success you and Augusta have led our mother to expect of a debutante, and it seems to be addling her mind. Or the family coffers have run dry. One or the other. Do you have any suggestions?

Belle smiled. That was certainly to the point but would also lead to difficulty if it were to land in her mother's hands at some point.

Dearest Florence,

I hope you and your little ones are doing well. We have enjoyed your detailed descriptions of your growing children immensely. It helps us to feel as though we can know them despite the long wait between visits. Thank you for keeping up such excellent correspondence.

That was just the right note to strike, Belle congratulated herself with a smile.

My debut has not been the most rousing of successes. It would seem our mother expected me to receive several offers on the very first day. This has not happened, much to her disappointment. I wouldn't be dreadfully disappointed if I were to wait another year as I don't find myself as eager as one would expect to get on with my adult life. Did you ever experience such a hesitation? I fear the terrible disappointment our parents will surely feel even while I cannot understand why there might be any sort of urgency to my marriage.

Perhaps it is the slight taint of my memories being those of a child, but I don't recall either you or our other sister ever having such pressure placed upon your betrothal. Was it you who was so eager to wed or our mother who wished to see you secured?

Belle wished she actually had pen and paper so she could write down what she wished to say right away. But, of course, she couldn't do that with her mother right across from her—besides the mess she would surely make if she tried to get out an inkwell in a moving carriage.

With a sigh, she assured herself she wasn't likely to forget her thoughts that quickly. It was an urgent enough matter; it wasn't as though it would slip from her mind. Especially not with Lady Bathurst berating her at every turn.

"You ought to be reading Debretts or practicing your needlework," Lady Bathurst interrupted her daughter's thoughts, almost as though she had read them.

Belle blinked. "In the moving carriage? Surely, I would get more blood on the fabric than threads pulled through."

"You should be skilled enough for that not to happen, I would think, if you had practiced sufficiently."

Now Belle was certain her mother was addled in the head. In all her life, Belle had never seen her mother try to do any sewing or needlework in a moving carriage. Not even in an unmoving carriage, for that matter. As far as she knew, all the needles and such were packed away. She supposed, if they were so inclined, they could knit, but she had never taken up that occupation. It would be safer, though, she would suppose. But it was a little too late to be lamenting her lack of training now.

Smoothing her hands over the gently worn brocade of the cushion beneath her helped Belle to keep her composure while she tried to pay just enough attention to her mother so as not to cause further irritation to that woman but not so much as to allow it to irritate herself. Finally, Lady Bathurst came to the conclusion of her latest lecture and settled back into the seat next to her husband.

Belle returned her attention to the passing scenery and allowed her mind to drift back to the past few weeks. It had been an exciting two weeks even if she didn't end up betrothed as her parents so clearly wished. Not to say that the house party was uncommonly exceptional. But the three betrothals that occurred ensured Lady Adelaide's status as a successful hostess on her very first attempt. She would never have to wonder if anyone would accept her invitation in the future.

Of course, as Viscountess Adelaide, married to the heir to the Earldom of Everleigh, it was doubtful she would ever have anyone refuse her invitation. But now it was doubly assured.

And she truly was happy for all three couples. Lady Constance, especially, if she were being honest. Since the lady had already lived a life that she loved and was a little older than the usual young woman fresh from the schoolroom making her debut. And of course, Lady Constance's soon-to-be sister-in-law Miss Alcott, or rather Mistress Northcott, since they had wed before all the guests had left Everleigh.

The wedding had been lovely. Belle hadn't attended an overabundance of weddings so she didn't have a great deal to compare them to. She hadn't even been allowed to go to Town for her sisters' weddings so she had only ever witnessed the ones held in the village church. But the eagerness with which they had wed was exciting to see.

Belle was a trifle envious. Even though she wasn't in any sort of rush to wed herself, seeing how delighted Mr. Northcott was to make Daisy his wife had warmed her heart. That was what she wanted for herself. Not just to wed with the first gentleman who offered so that her parents could be satisfied for whatever reason seemed to be troubling them.

The long drive was wearying, and it seemed to Belle that her parents were acting strangely, exchanging glances every now and then that seemed unusual. She wasn't sure if it was her exhaustion making her suspicious or if they really were acting furtive. She closed her eyes to rest for a few minutes.

A sudden, loud cracking sound brought her firmly awake, confused by her fatigue and the now tilting position of the carriage.

Chapter Two

Robert Francis Scranton, fifth Viscount Simmons, was tired. It seemed as though his fatigue went even deeper than his bones, which was an odd and fanciful thought. Yes, he had ridden all the way, but even his horse seemed fine despite the long journey, and really, he had been the one doing all the work.

Rob thought it was perhaps a matter of the mind or heart, and he wasn't really prepared to contemplate that sort of thing. He had no interest in engaging his heart. Not to say that he aspired to be heartless, but his flighty mother was forever spouting about matters of the heart, and Robert wanted nothing to do with such things.

Perhaps that was why the Season was such a chore.

Of course, he was well aware that he needed to wed. He did wish to do so. He wasn't one of these silly fops who wished to remain a bachelor for life. He wanted his future settled and his duty to produce an heir taken care of so he could just get on with living. Robert had never enjoyed anything unsettled, and right now, it felt as though his entire existence was a morass of unsettled matters.

But it was also not a matter to be rushed into. The future Viscountess Simmons had a serious role to fill. Rob didn't feel his mother had been the very best choice for that role despite the fact that he loved her dearly, for the most part. Perhaps that was why he was so resistant to allowing his heart into the matter. It had been evident to Rob from a young age that his father had been very much in love with his wife despite the fact that she had moved out of the family home for a large chunk of Robert's young life. It hadn't struck young Rob as a comfortable state to be in, especially when it went wrong. In the case of his parents, despite their reconciling and producing two more children, Robert didn't consider their so-called love match to be something to emulate. He would much rather a civilized union that never left any children wondering what had happened to their mother.

And having witnessed two rather emotional couplings take place, nearly right in front of his eyes, had convinced Robert further that it was not a situation he cared to find himself in.

But ladies seemed more and more convinced that they wanted a love match.

Robert had heard it said that most members of the *ton* decried such a situation. He had always understood that adults agreed that marriage amongst the members of Society was more of a business arrangement than a heart engagement. But the debutantes were getting younger and younger in his mind, and they didn't seem to have been taught that important fact.

Even the two most recently betrothed young women of Society, who weren't even that terribly young, had seemed delighted to have found a love match even though Robert would have sworn that both of them were far too sensible for such a thing when he had first made their acquaintance. In addition, Lady Constance's companion, the future Lady Merton, had seemed even more sensible than most.

But then there was the beautiful but young Lady Isabelle who had also been at the house party he had just left. She didn't seem particularly interested in either the business or the emotional side of making a marriage contract. It had been her father who had assessed him from the tips of his toes to the top of his head and seemed to estimate every last farthing Robert owned to his name. It wasn't unusual, he supposed. It was a father's prerogative and even his duty to ensure his daughter was going to be well provided for. But it had been off-putting that the young lady hadn't seemed the least bit interested.

And now he was being even more ridiculous because he also didn't like it when a lady very obviously set her cap at him. He couldn't have it both ways. Either she was obvious or she wasn't. Robert supposed he was looking for something in the middle, but that was evidently asking too much as he hadn't yet been able to discover this type of unique woman.

Much to his surprise, the sound of knocking could be heard throughout his small house. *Well, small might be the wrong word for it,* Robert thought with a grin as he glanced around. Size was definitely a perspective matter. In comparison to Everleigh, the vast estate he had just been visiting, his hunting lodge was tiny. But when compared with even his bachelor's lodgings in Town, the lodge was spacious, large enough to host even the most discerning of guests.

But he wasn't expecting anyone. And as far as he knew, no one would even know that he was in residence as he had intended to return to Town and finish out the Parliamentary Season before returning to his estate. He had just needed a couple days to regroup and gather his thoughts before wading back into the whirl of life, never mind the assignment he was supposed to be taking care of. Town could wait briefly, but not for much longer.

The house party had unsettled him. He ought to have been the one finding his match rather than being left behind to envy those gentlemen who had done so.

Robert shook his head. He was talking himself in circles inside his mind. And it was leading him nowhere. It also didn't answer the question of who had been knocking on his door.

He wasn't left wondering long, though, as a footman came scratching on his door at that moment.

"My lord, there are guests to see you."

"To see me?" Robert asked. "Me specifically? Did you ask their names?"

"Yes, my lord, my apologies for not saying so right away. It's Lord and Lady Bathurst and their daughter; I believe they said—"

"Lady Isabelle," Robert finished for him as he stood with a frown. "How…" He wanted to say odd but didn't want to disrespect his noble guests in front of his servants. "Interesting," he completed rather lamely. But it *was* interesting. Why would they stop in at his lodge? Was this a ruse? The earl and his wife had made no secret of the fact that they would consider him an eligible match for their lovely daughter. But Robert hadn't pursued the matter at the house party beyond the most surface-deep of inquiries.

Were they hoping to entrap him? Or perhaps just convince him more privately without the distraction of others? There was only one way to find out, he thought as he followed the footman from the room after a quick glance in the mirror above the mantle in his library.

He might not be dressed at the height of fashion, as was his wont, but they would surely realise he had been travelling all day much as they had. And he had not been expecting guests, he reminded himself.

"Lord Simmons, do forgive the imposition," Lord Bathurst greeted him jovially as soon as he stepped foot into the room they had been shown to. "Would you believe our carriage wheel broke just steps from your door?"

"It was most fortuitous," the man's wife insisted on the heels of Lord Bathurst's words. "Imagine if we had been far from any sort of civilisation? And with evening setting in? I don't know what would have become of us. But my dear Lord Bathurst immediately recognised where we were and was certain you would be happy to help us out."

Robert was hard pressed to keep his amusement from showing when his gaze took in the assembled trio. Lord and Lady Bathurst appeared cheerful and delighted over the turn of events while their daughter looked as though she was contemplating leaping from the nearest window. His curiosity was piqued.

"Of course," he finally answered. He wasn't happy to have his home invaded by these obviously encroaching guests, but there was very little else he could say in response. Short of turning them out into the night, he would have to accept their presence in what he had hoped would be quiet solitude.

"Have my servants made you comfortable? I suppose I ought to apologise that I don't have a great number of them. This was an unexpected stop for me and, as you can imagine, we weren't expecting guests."

"You don't appear to have a butler," Lady Bathurst said with some distaste before her husband caught her eye, and she struggled to turn her frown into a smile. "But the footman was perfectly polite as he showed us into this quaint little room to wait for you."

Now, an encompassing glance around the room showed that Lady Isabelle had paled further and appeared torn between anger and mortification. Robert was all the more reluctantly intrigued. He could not rid himself of them, at least for the night, so he would do his best to be amused rather than irritated.

It was likely an attempt to entrap him into the parson's mousetrap. He had never seen it tried with both parents present, but how else could they have so conveniently had carriage problems right in front of his door such as they had?

"Have your servants gone for help for your carriage?" he thought to inquire. He really didn't want to be burdened with this group longer than the one night.

"Your man directed our driver where to go," Lord Bathurst spoke up. "I don't have any confidence that they'll be able to do anything before tomorrow, but at least they have gotten a start on it."

Rob had to work at keeping a frown off of his face. From Lord Bathurst's tone, it didn't sound overly conniving. But it was too pat of a coincidence for his liking.

"I don't suppose you've eaten," Robert said. "I'm sure my staff are scrambling something together. Have you any luggage? Would you like to be shown to some rooms so you can freshen up?"

Again Lady Isabelle made a small sound of distress, almost undetectable, to the point that no one else in the room reacted in the least, but

Robert couldn't help looking at her. She hid it well, but he could tell she was acutely uncomfortable. Whether it was the thought of their imposing upon him or the idea that she might not be perfectly presentable, Rob couldn't say in that moment. It would be interesting to see where the evening progressed, to say the least.

It might not be as interesting as puzzling over the latest correspondence from his contact at the Home Office, as he had been planning on doing, but as he had considered previously, there was really nothing else he could do but accept the situation at its face value and hope for the best. His investigation wasn't going to go anywhere on its own, so it could, unfortunately, wait another day or two, and he was fully confident that his estates were in good hands with the stewards in charge, so there wasn't really anything urgent he needed to attend to.

He did hate leaving correspondence unattended, though. He managed not to sigh audibly.

Chapter Three

Isabelle wanted to sink through the floor. She couldn't fathom how her parents had managed to engineer such an event, but surely the damage to the carriage must have been orchestrated in some way. She had seen with her own eyes that the wheel was damaged, so she was certain that was legitimate, but the fact that her mother had just been lamenting her failure to capture the viscount's attention was a little too well-timed for her comfort. And then to find themselves quite literally on his doorstep? Far too cringeworthy for her.

But what could she do short of throwing herself out the window? And what good would that do? She'd be all the more ruined.

Could they really think to threaten her with ruin? The sudden thought chilled her blood.

No, surely they were merely trying to arrange a private viewing, as it were. A chance for Lord Simmons to get to know her in the comfort of his own home, perhaps? She could only hope so since the alternative idea of their trying to see her reputation ruined wasn't even possible for her to contemplate.

And the man was surely suspicious. The way he had looked at them all when he'd first entered the room made her feel lower than the dust under his feet. Which had made her bristle for the briefest moment. But she couldn't hold her head up when she imagined what her parents had done. If only the floor would conveniently open up and swallow her upon command, she could be comfortable. That thought brought a brief moment of relief from utter mortification as she pondered her wish. Would one really be comfortable if swallowed by the floor? Perhaps comfortable was the wrong word, but it would surely be better than this.

But no, she had to endure her parents' less-than-subtle subterfuge under the haughty nose of Viscount Simmons. Her misery was complete.

Except she wasn't the miserable sort, she reminded herself. Isabelle had never been the dramatic type. Her feelings didn't run nearly as hot or cold as some of her more volatile friends. She had never had a fit of the vapors. Although, this would be the time for it if she was so inclined, she thought with the first glimmer of amusement she had been able to muster since she had felt the carriage lurch so sickeningly.

"This way, please, my lady," the footman called her scattering wits into place as he led her and her parents from the room. To freshen their appearance. What a fop the viscount was. As though her appearance was of the least concern when they had just had a carriage accident.

Of course, she was well aware that appearances mattered. And if her parents were so desperate to marry her off that they would stage a broken carriage wheel, then she ought to do what she could to work along with their plans.

But Isabelle was also aware that the foppish-seeming Viscount Simmons was not a stupid man. He'd had suspicion painted on his features when he had been shown into the receiving room her family had been settled in. Belle was actually surprised he hadn't directly said anything.

The man had been perfectly polite, at least on the surface of the situation. But Belle had still been entirely uncomfortable. Hopefully, it would only be until the next day. Perhaps, on the furthest stretch of the imagination, the carriage wheel really had broken at the opportune time, and it was merely a matter of having it fixed, and they could be on their way with an amusing story to tell.

Everyone had travel adventures to tell about. If one didn't live in London full-time, then there were perils to be faced in getting to the capital for the Season. She had heard all sorts of tales of inn debacles as well as dreadful roads and any other manner of adventure. Isabelle had been fortunate not to have experienced any such thing herself thus far in her life.

Until now, that was. But was it truly an accident?

That was the big question she endured. But she could barely face the viscount.

Before she had time to do anything other than run a comb through her hair and splash some water on her face, Lady Bathurst was at the door, urging her to hurry to return to Lord Simmons' company.

"A golden opportunity has landed right in your lap, and you'd best not waste it, this time, Isabelle. I cannot fathom why you have been such a failure up until now. You are pretty, well-trained, and exceptionally dowered. You should have been the first to become betrothed, not the last."

"I do not see why you are in such a hurry to see the back of me, Mother. Surely there is no need for this urgency."

"It is time," was all her mother would say, not the least bit helpful in clearing the confusion in Belle's mind, as she twitched the skirts of her daughter's gown in a critical fashion. "You should have worn the brocade," she complained before adding, "You'll do." That was a relief to Isabelle as there were no other options. The carriage with their luggage and servants had gone ahead of them and was likely already arriving in Town.

Being the steady-natured girl that she was, up until now, she hadn't been all that worked up over the matter of her mother insisting she needed to wed soon. Aside from the embarrassment of being so dreadfully obvious before Lord Simmons at the house party, Belle had almost laughed about her mother's seeming desperation to marry her off. She hadn't actually believed her mother was so serious on the topic prior to the house party. Now, though, she was mortified to be thrust at the viscount in such an obvious way. It struck her as the very epitome of every tall tale she had ever heard of match-making mamas and their unattractive daughters. It made her feel as though her parents thought her unacceptable in some way if they were that eager to be rid of her. It was a lowering sensation, to be sure.

"Smile, girl," her mother practically hissed as Isabelle allowed her thoughts to drift. "You can't catch flies with vinegar."

"But who would ever wish to catch flies?" Isabelle countered, refusing to cow herself to her mother's seeming anger.

"I'm older and wiser than you, Isabelle; you'd do much better to listen to me."

"I know, Mother, but you have put me in a decidedly awkward situation."

Lady Bathurst couldn't quite meet her eye, but she wasn't willing to concede anything. "I have no idea what you are going on about," she protested. "You couldn't possibly be suggesting that our being stranded here was some sort of stratagem, could you?"

Isabelle opened her mouth to argue, but before she could, she thought better of it. What could she prove? And if they were to be overheard, it could be considered the height of scandal. And what could be accomplished by that?

Nothing.

Whether it had been done on purpose or not, there was no getting around the fact that they were there now. Lord Simmons had not refused them his hospitality, and for at least one night, they would be his guests. If there was a merciful god in the heavens, then early the next morning, their carriage would be fixed, and they could carry on about their travels without any breath of scandal touching upon them and the viscount put to the least trouble.

Or they might end up ensconced in his home for days.

A shiver travelled through Isabelle. The very thought made her wonder if the roof of the lodge was high enough for her to jump off and end the mortification. That thought brought her up short, and she nearly stumbled over her feet even as she followed her mother to the room they had been received in earlier.

She was a reasonably intelligent young lady. Whatever her parents' machinations might be, surely she could avoid succumbing to their schemes, especially if the gentleman was also not favouring a match.

Her stomach might tie itself in knots, but there was no need to contemplate her own demise, Belle assured herself with a surge of anger.

Her anger helped her get through the rest of the evening.

She was primarily angry with her parents for putting her in this awkward position, and at herself for reacting in such an overwrought way, but she had enough anger to direct some of it at the viscount. He might be their unwilling host, but he needn't be sneery about it, she thought as she sipped at the glass of excellent wine the footman had just poured.

Was sneery a word?

Belle's eyes widened. How many glasses had she been served? Had she allowed her anger to distract her enough that she had drunk too much wine?

Ever since she was quite young, Isabelle had known to limit her wine, and she never partook of anything stronger. She wasn't sure if it was because she was small or because she was young, but she couldn't seem to enjoy it the way others could.

And now, she was reasonably sure she had allowed herself to have a little too much. And she had been too angry to even enjoy it.

If she kept her mouth shut, no one would have to know. And that would be easy as Lady Bathurst had kept the conversation going steady ever since the viscount had shown up in the receiving room.

Lord Simmons had been dressed as though he were going to a formal gathering in Town rather than a casual supper at his lodge. Isabelle wondered if it was his intention to make them feel travel-worn and dirty. Whether he did it on purpose or not, that was the result, for her, at least.

He was one of the most beautiful men she had ever seen. She couldn't decide if that was appealing or not. She was leaning toward thinking it was unappealing. Who would want a husband prettier than herself?

Not to say that he appeared effeminate in any way. She didn't know another man who could pull off some of the colours he wore. There was just something about his wide shoulders and square jaw that made it work for him. No one could mistake he was a man, even if he were to turn up in a gown. She had to press her lips together to stifle a snort of laughter at the image that came to her mind on that errant thought.

But she wasn't certain if he could ever be the man for her, even if her parents were able to scheme their way into a marriage contract. That thought made Isabelle's anger ratchet up another notch, but this time, it was directed squarely at herself. She had allowed herself to get into a compromised position. At least intellectually compromised. Her hands clenched together where she had placed them in her lap, and she took a deep breath to control her thoughts and mounting anger at everyone present, herself included.

A quick mental scan of herself assured Isabelle that she wasn't as far gone as she had first thought. Yes, it had been foolish to lose track of what she was eating and drinking, but the damage wasn't too bad. Perhaps a little more meat and potatoes, and she might be just fine.

Her wits were definitely required. It had been witless of her to allow them to be dispersed.

That thought made amusement battle with her anger as she imagined a dog scattering her wits like it might a flock of sheep. She blinked her eyes a couple times, hoping no one would notice her diminished capacities. Or at least they would attribute it to fatigue. What a backward mistake to make. Belle studiously avoided meeting anyone's gaze as she smiled toward the footman who was offering her another serving. She was stuffed from the meal already, but she couldn't seem to stop herself. Clearly Lord Simmons even chose his staff well. Belle sighed gently.

Chapter Four

Robert was torn in his feelings as he watched Lady Isabelle struggle for control.

She had seemed lividly angry when he'd arrived in the receiving room right before his footman had announced that supper would be served in the dining room. Although he wasn't completely certain to whom the anger was directed. It was perhaps just general irritation with everyone. Robert couldn't help admiring the proud and belligerent tilt to the young woman's chin. And her high colour only served to highlight the brilliance of her grey gaze as she stared defiantly at whomever spoke.

She added very little to the conversation. Robert wasn't sure if that was because Lady Bathurst barely stopped for breath. He also wasn't certain how the older woman managed to eat with all her chatter, but she was somehow able to put away a surprising amount of his cook's excellent food despite her small frame.

In between glaring at all the other occupants of the room except the servants, Lady Isabelle took small, delicate bites that Robert found strangely appealing. Despite the seeming ferocity of the anger she was unable to hide, she still managed to eat like a delicate, dainty princess. Not that Robert had ever seen a princess eat as all the royal sons had chosen not to yet wed, but it was how he would imagine a princess or a fairy sprite would eat.

He almost shook his head. His odd reactions to the sudden arrival of Bathurst and his family were addling his mind, evidently. Fairy sprites? From where had that ridiculous idea sprung? Robert allowed amusement to touch his face, if only to see if Lady Isabelle would actually burst into flames from the heat of her anger.

It amused him, too, to watch her continue to sip at her wine as though she didn't even notice she was doing so. Being such a small woman, it was sure to lead her into trouble. He hoped it would loosen her tongue as he longed to hear her express the colourful thoughts that were clearly traipsing through her head.

What could have made her so angry? And why was her anger so indiscriminate? She didn't seem to harbour any ill will towards his servants so she wasn't just a cranky person from the long drive. It was specific to himself and her parents. Perhaps others, as well, who weren't present. But the fact that she was not just generally angry intrigued Robert far more than he would like.

He wanted to despise the woman, but he found that quite impossible. It was more than irritating.

What was he going to do with these uninvited guests? He tried to turn his attention back to Lady Bathurst but she was far from interesting.

"Will you be returning to take your seat for the rest of Parliament?" Lady Bathurst had finally landed on something he might enjoy talking about.

"Yes, I am anxious to return as there is a bill I wish to support."

Lady Bathurst's knowing nod set his teeth on edge.

"Perhaps we could travel to Town together, in that case, as my lord Bathurst is also in a hurry to return."

"Only if your carriage is repaired, of course," Robert murmured with a glance toward Lady Isabelle from the corner of his eye.

The poor young woman looked like she wished to spit at him like a young kitten who had been removed too soon from its milk. Rob didn't even bother to suppress his amusement.

"Well, if you wished to offer us a spot in your carriage, surely we wouldn't be troubled by our wheel if it weren't repaired too quickly."

Robert gritted his teeth. "We shall see how it progresses on the morrow," was all he could say. He had less than no desire to have the earl and his wife and daughter in his company any longer than he was required by human decency to do. That was surely restricted to one night. This night. He would offer them to break their fast in the morning, and then he would urge them out the door. Surely they could be accommodated in the nearest village and he needn't put himself out any more than he had already done.

But then he saw Lady Isabelle realise she had drunk too much of his best wine. The expression on her face was the most amusing and endearing he had ever witnessed.

Despite the odd circumstances, he wasn't having the worst time. That honour still remained whenever his mother visited him in recent times. Her quest to ensure the lineage was driving him to feel like a candidate for Bedlam. Her determination to see him wed was almost ensuring that he do the very opposite of what she was asking of him. Which also was driving him mad. He hated the thought of his being so dismally illogical. He knew he had to ensure the lineage. He didn't need to be told so by his mother who hadn't set the best example on that score with her leaving her husband for almost a decade. Feeling so illogical made him feel the need to exert control in every aspect of his life. But it also made him feel like rebelling. And, so, he dressed in higher and higher fashion to the point that he knew himself to appear as a fop, and it irritated his mother so. It was most ridiculous.

Amusement rose in him again. He supposed he was still a rebellious toddler if one judged him by his actions. He ought to offer his uninvited guests as much empathy or at least a modicum of understanding as he tried to do for himself whenever he did odd things.

Even if they were trying to entrap him, he didn't have to fall into the trap, now, did he? Surely if he could see it coming, he could avoid it quite handily.

He might not be a scholar, but surely he wasn't a dunce either.

And so it was that he tried to engage Lady Isabelle in conversation.

"What did you enjoy best about your time at Everleigh?"

His innocuous question earned him a glare. But then she closed her eyes. Or perhaps it was just a very long blink, he thought with a smile as suddenly her eyes popped open and she looked at him with her intelligent, if slightly glazed, grey gaze.

"I would say it was the people," she finally said in a slightly louder than usual voice but with all her words properly enunciated. Robert was impressed.

"Could you elaborate, my dear? Do you mean meeting new people? I would have thought you would have already been introduced to everyone there."

Her smile, when she wasn't glaring at him, was bright and cheery. Robert wondered if it was the wine or if that was her usual temperament that had somehow been dampened at the party.

"I had already met everyone with the exception of Lady Constance and Miss Smith. But I found the atmosphere more relaxed than at a usual Society event. As a result, people were more relaxed. I'm not certain if you could say they were more themselves, but I did find some of them easier to get to know. But perhaps that was merely because there was more time spent together." She shook her head and looked adorably embarrassed. "I'm not explaining this at all well. It was almost like having neighbours. You know how you are much better acquainted with your neighbours at home than ever you are with people in Town? That's how it felt."

Robert smiled and was sorry to see that his smile irritated her and her frown returned. He had enjoyed her response even if it was a trifle garbled. Of course, as a debutante, her situation would be different than his. Having come up to London many times, he felt as though he knew other members of the *ton* nearly as well as he did his neighbours in the village near his estate, but he understood what she meant. When you'd been acquainted with people your entire life, it was a much different story than meeting someone at a Society event.

"Does that mean you aren't enjoying your Season overmuch or just that you quite enjoyed your time at Everleigh?" Robert tried to pry into the workings of her mind, but to his surprise, his question prompted another glare for the entire room.

"Neither, in all honesty," she finally answered. "But I did enjoy spending time out of doors at Everleigh. It felt a little more like home than anything else. Not to say that I have a home." She concluded her short speech with another pointed glare toward her mother, and suddenly, Robert thought he understood.

It would seem the young lady wasn't as anxious as she ought to be to leave home. It was seeming less and less likely that she was involved in whatever plot her parents might have to entrap him, if there even was a trap. Robert quickly corrected himself. Of course, she was involved since she was one of the parties, but she wasn't in agreement. He found that comforting to a degree. It was still an awkward situation in which to find himself, but it was far more amusing in these circumstances. He was curious to see how far her lack of willingness would take her.

Robert was just about to ask the footmen to bring in some other beverage like lemonade or something when his thought processes were interrupted by the sound of a commotion coming from the foyer. Surprise had him casting a frown at his head footman who hurried from the room to intercept the problem. Robert swallowed a sigh. He never would have thought he would wish for more servants at his hunting lodge.

The sound of raised, youthful voices wafted through the closed dining room door, and Robert had a momentary shaft of pleasure as he watched Lady Isabelle's befuddled anger shift to curiosity. Her expression no longer held irritation as she looked to him in inquiry.

"You don't have children, do you?" she asked innocently.

"Don't let them hear you speak of them as children," he whispered loudly with a wink. "If I'm not mistaken, that is my brother and sister. While I don't exactly have children of my own, as Viscount Simmons, I am responsible for them.

Especially when they become excessively irritated with our mother, I find they come running to me."

She smiled at him before she appeared to remember that she was angry, and she blinked away her pleasant expression into one that was far more neutral, but he was relieved to see that she didn't appear so furious, at least not with him.

Robert had no more time to contemplate Lady Isabelle as the door was suddenly thrust open, and his young siblings strode into the room with the footman on their heels.

"Robert, I told Sutton you would want to see us and that I didn't believe you had company." His sister's strident voice filled the room even as she came to a sudden halt and hot colour splashed upon her cheeks.

"But now you can see that he wasn't lying to you," Robert replied mildly, even as he rose to his feet. "Might I present Lady Bathurst, Lord Bathurst, and their daughter Lady Isabelle?"

Lucretia and Cuthbert, his two, much younger siblings, looking bashful as only teenagers could, remembered their manners and bowed and curtsied correctly.

"How do you do?" was murmured by all in the room.

"But you never said you'd be having company. You just said you'd be stopping here to rest before you continued on to Town, and so we thought it would be best to find you here."

"You will have to excuse us for interfering with whatever you had planned, Miss Scranton, as our arrival was not expected," Lady Isabelle surprised Robert by politely replying. "Is your matter so urgent that we ought to leave the room? Or can it wait until after we've finished dining?"

His sister's face was a contrast in emotions. She was nearly struck dumb from Isabelle's beauty and poise. She was also seemingly rather cowed by the obvious issue that her matter was not the least bit urgent and they shouldn't have burst upon him while he was dining. But his young sister also clearly wished to be sophisticated and correct.

"No, no, there's no need for you to interrupt your meal. We shouldn't have burst upon you like we did. We can withdraw until you are finished."

Lady Isabelle surprised him again. She glanced in his direction from beneath her lashes, but then she ignored the rest of the room except his siblings.

"I cannot guess how far you've travelled, but I must ask, have you eaten? While the kitchens weren't prepared for even our arrival, it is likely there is enough to spare a little for the two of you if you'd care to join us."

Lucy rightly glanced down at her gown and then at her brother, but Isabelle waved away her evident concerns.

"We arrived in our travel clothes, as well; it cannot be helped," she said with a smile that seemed to put his brother and sister at ease. They appeared happy to take their seat in chairs the footmen were quick to pull forward for them.

Robert was befuddled by the turn of events. He hadn't seen the youngsters in a couple of months but corresponded with each of them regularly. He also often heard from their tutor and their mother. Before he could pursue questioning them, though, Lady Bathurst had zeroed in on his sister and was politely interrogating her. What amused him the most, though, was Lady Isabelle's less than subtle efforts to lessen the impact of her mother's questions on the younger girl. He could have told her that, after her lifetime of experience with their own mother, his sister could take whatever her mother threw at her, but it was far more amusing to watch it all play out.

Chapter Five

Her anger at the situation she found herself in was suddenly forgotten, at least for the moment. While it was likely that it would return if she thought too long about the situation she had been thrust into by her parents' probable scheming and the viscount's indifference, now there were two others who were in more need of attention than she was.

Isabelle tried to keep her mouth shut, but she just couldn't manage it. The young pair that had just arrived seemed to change everything. The boy barely said a word, but that might be because he was clearly ravenous. As the youngest sibling, Belle didn't have the same perspective as she did now, but she could somewhat remember her brothers at this age. It seemed to be a universal trait to be endlessly hungry. It was actually rather endearing. She couldn't prevent her gaze from shifting to their unwilling host as she wondered what he had been like at a similar age.

There wasn't a strong resemblance between the siblings, but the tilt of their eyes and the colour of their hair did mark them as family. She also wondered about the obvious age difference. Perhaps there were other siblings in between, and just this pair had turned up unannounced.

Belle was impressed with her mother's restraint. It had to be disappointing to have the extra family members show up to add to the resistance to whatever scheme her parents had planned. Instead, though, it seemed to Belle as though her mother was almost pleased with the development.

One more piece of evidence that she would never understand her mother.

It was odd as she had used to think they were reasonably close. As close as one could be to a woman who had kept her distance for most of her childhood. Belle had been raised by maids and governesses, it seemed to her, with only an occasional visit to the drawing room to demonstrate to the well-dressed adults what she had been learning. In their family, it wasn't until you were at least thirteen or more years old that you could graduate to dining with the grown-ups on occasion. And so it was that, one by one, her siblings had disappeared from the nursery wing of the house. Her brothers, of course, had left for school, rarely to return. And then her sisters had made their debut, never to return. Until it had been just her left at Bathurst with her parents who seemed far more interested in each other and their personal pursuits than in their youngest child who was struggling with feelings of having been abandoned by everyone in her life.

Could that really be why they were in such a hurry to see her wed? They just wanted to concern themselves with each other rather than with anyone who might be dependent upon them? Belle tried not to think about that. There were other things of concern now.

Watching Lord Simmons pay close attention to whatever his brother and sister had to say filled her with a deep longing that she fought to ignore. She didn't want to be his sibling. She didn't want to be his anything, she reminded herself.

Her parents had schemed to have themselves and her there. Whatever they had planned had obviously been interrupted, but they didn't seem overly put out by it. From what Belle could tell, her father was only interested in the fine claret being poured into his cup regularly while she was relieved that the servants had brought much lighter beverages with the arrival of the youngsters. She happily allowed lemonade to be added to her glass, as well.

The foggy feeling her brain had been filled with earlier was slowly dissipating, and for the most part, she was able to concentrate on everything around her. It was a lot to take in, though. Between the handsome man at the end of the table seemingly all-knowing and the happy chatter filling the room, from Lady Bathurst's skilled questioning of the viscount's sister, Belle wasn't sure where to rest her gaze.

"Have you been sent down from school?" she asked the boy, who was sitting closest to her, as quietly as possible.

He ducked his head and glanced at her from the corner of his eye.

"I didn't go this year," he answered her quietly.

"Oh, were you relieved or disappointed?" She didn't mean to pry, but she was truly curious. Belle had always thought it was unfair that her brothers got to go away to school but she and her sisters didn't, save for a few weeks at the nearby "finishing" school run by the ever-so-proper Miss Daniels.

The boy beside her ducked his head, grinning and shaking his head. That didn't communicate much of an answer to her, so she waited to see if he would finally say something.

"I suppose a bit of both," he finally said in a low voice after glancing toward his brother as though to make sure he couldn't hear what they were saying.

"I guess I can understand that. It's much like my Season. I'm happy to make my debut, and yet, I would rather be at home."

"Really?" The boy's wide, blue gaze was now watchful and no longer darting around as though he were too nervous to look directly at her. "I would think you would be very good at such things."

That shed some light for Isabelle. She thought perhaps he was nervous at school because he either wasn't successful academically or socially.

"I'm not particularly good at it, in all honesty. But I'm not sure if that's a symptom or the cause of why I would rather be home. Perhaps I'm not all that successful because others can guess that I am not that enthusiastic. Or perhaps I'd rather be at home because I'm not being very successful." She grinned and winked at the boy. "It's a quandary. Which do you suppose it is?"

The boy stared as though he couldn't fathom for a moment, but then his gaze sharpened. "I don't suppose it's a lack of interest on your part. In my experience, boys want what they can't have, so I would expect disinterest on your part to make you all the more interesting to the gentlemen."

Far from offended, Isabelle couldn't help grinning at the youngster. "Thank you, Mr. Cuthbert. I appreciate your assistance on the matter. You are quite easy to talk to. I almost wish you were in Town for the Season, but I don't really want to wish that upon you."

"And I'm far too young anyhow," he replied promptly with a grin. "But it's kind of you to say so." Again he glanced at his brother. "I don't suppose Simmons would wish for me to be there anyhow."

"He seemed quite happy to see you despite the surprise," Belle answered mildly, unsure of the family dynamics.

"He's exceedingly polite."

Belle laughed lightly. "Such a degree of politeness can seem terrible at times, can't it?"

Cuthbert nodded vigorously.

"Why do you suppose he is that way?" she couldn't prevent herself from asking despite the fact that it seemed somewhat underhanded to be asking the viscount's young brother about him.

"Probably to keep us all at a distance."

"Well, yes, but why would he wish to do that?"

"I reckon it's on account of his inheriting too young."

Belle smiled over the boy's wording. He had likely heard the sentiment many times.

"You might be right," she commented, unable to imagine taking on so much responsibility at a young age. She couldn't really imagine taking it on now, let alone if she were a youngster as Lord Simmons must have been when his father died. And now, meeting his siblings, she saw that the responsibility would have been even greater than she had originally imagined.

"Do you have any other brothers and sisters?" she asked quietly. If she had done as her mother had suggested in the carriage and reread her Debretts, she might know the answer to this question.

"No, just us three," Cuthbert answered just as quietly. "I'm the spare," he added in a matter-of-fact tone. "They had given up for a while, it would seem. Then they got Lucy and tried again for me."

Belle blinked, unsure what to say. "I'm sure your parents were delighted by the arrival of all three of their children," she said as firmly as she could given her own murky relationship with her parents.

"Do you have many brothers and sisters?"

"I'm one of six," Belle answered. "I have three brothers and two sisters. Like you, I'm the youngest."

"Do you hate it?" he asked.

"Being the youngest? Or having so many brothers and sisters?"

The boy shrugged as though he didn't care about her answer or her question but then glanced up the table toward Lord Simmons once more before leaning closer and saying, "Being the youngest," in the lowest voice he could manage.

Belle lifted a shoulder in a half shrug, unsure how to answer his question. "Hate is a pretty strong word and, of course, I don't know what it might be like to fall elsewhere in the family order, but it's not my favourite. It does feel to me as though I am being treated differently than my sisters were, and that irritates me considerably." She paused for a moment and then added with a laugh, "But I also wish I had been born a boy. Neither wishes are going to be granted."

The boy laughed along with her, nodding in agreement. "Why do you think it would be better to be a boy?"

"Dressing would be easier, for one thing," Isabelle replied promptly with a grin.

Again the boy glanced at his brother. "I'm not so certain of that. I've seen my brother's valet helping him with his coat and such, and especially if he has to attend court. I don't think it's much easier for a gentleman than a lady."

Belle wrinkled her nose and fought a blush. She shouldn't have raised that particular questionable topic. "You also have way more freedom and I suspect, much more fun than girls."

"That might be true," the boy answered with a nod and a grin. "Not that my sister has any interest in my activities, but I consider them far more interesting than hers."

Belle laughed, enjoying the boy's sense of humour. She was surprised to feel the viscount's gaze on her. She raised her eyebrows in his direction. She couldn't bolster her anger any longer, not in the youngsters' presence. But she wasn't ready to be overly friendly with her host or her parents either.

Lady Bathurst got to her feet, startling everyone in the room.

"Ought we to leave the gentlemen to their port, ladies?"

Isabelle almost allowed her jaw to drop open. Her mother was going to stand on such ceremony with only six people in residence, one of them a schoolboy? And this a hunting lodge? After she swallowed her surprise, she also had to fight against hysterical laughter. The entire sojourn at Lord Simmons' place was turning into more and more of a farce, and she was unsure how to extricate herself.

But short of causing a scene, she had to follow her mother's lead after she proposed their departure. And the viscount's sister seemed thrilled with the turn of events so Belle smiled at the girl and followed her mother from the room while avoiding Lord Simmons' watchful gaze. Belle didn't think she could meet his eye and keep her chin up as she had been doing thus far that evening. With the protection of her anger diminished by her conversation with young Cuthbert, there was nothing for her to do but ignore him. Perhaps there had been no reason to be angry in the first place, and now, she felt completely exposed without it.

"The servants brought your needlework if you'd like to be properly occupied, Isabelle," Lady Bathurst said, eliciting a small snort from her less-than-fond daughter.

"Isn't that fortuitous," Belle answered with light sarcasm, wondering where they had found it considering the carriage with their personal servants and luggage had gone ahead of them, unaware of their accident. "While they were at it, did they manage to procure a new wheel for the carriage?"

"I have been informed that might take a little longer."

Belle was surprised her mother was able to keep a straight face while making her statement.

"Was it very dreadful?" Lucretia asked.

"Was what dreadful, my dear?" Lady Bathurst asked before Belle could formulate a comment.

"The carriage accident. I have never been in an accident so I am curious."

Belle had to cough to cover her huff of laughter, curious to find out how her mother would answer the question.

"It wasn't remarkably dramatic. And we were so fortunate to be close to your brother's property so we were able to find shelter quite quickly. That was my biggest fear, being stuck on an unfamiliar road overnight."

The girl shuddered dramatically. "That *would* be horrible."

Isabelle realised she ought to step into the conversation lest the girl's awe over the matter encourage Lady Bathurst in her own dramatics.

"Did you have far to travel today?" Belle asked the girl.

Miss Lucretia sighed dramatically. "I have no idea how far it was, but we were in that carriage for hours. That is why I worry about having an accident similar to yours. It was probably because you were driving for so long, right? Have the men figured out what caused it?"

The girl's innocent question set Belle's teeth on edge. The implication that they couldn't figure out for themselves what had happened merely because they were women irritated her to no end. While it was no doubt the expected way of things, Belle bristled against it, determined not to be dismissed merely due to her gender.

She couldn't argue that she was stronger than a man in a physical sense, but she was reasonably confident her mind worked as well or better. Belle bit back the smile that threatened to spill over onto her face when she wondered how Lord Simmons would react to her thoughts on the matter. Not that she was likely to ever find out. And, she reminded herself that determined not to fall for her mother's machinations, she didn't care much for the gentleman's thoughts anyhow.

Belle tried to revive the righteous anger that had gotten her through the early part of the evening but fatigue combined with her enjoyment of the newly arrived young additions to their gathering and she was feeling far more mellow than she had been earlier.

Of course, she was still irritated with her parents but she realised it was foolish of her to be angry with Lord Simmons along with them. It wasn't as though he was in cahoots with them nor had he invited their invasion into his home. In fact, rather than being angry with him, she ought to have sympathy.

She didn't want to feel sympathy for the handsome man, though.

And so it was that she was in a highly conflicted state of mind when the gentlemen joined them in the receiving room.

"I do hope you were comfortable enough in here," Lord Simmons greeted them upon his arrival. "The servants here at my lodge are unaccustomed to the niceties of entertaining as I'm sure you can imagine."

Belle opened her mouth as though to answer even though she had no idea what her mind wished to say, but she was interrupted by Lord Simmons' sister before she could speak.

"Robert, don't be silly. You know full well there isn't a single servant in your employ who hasn't been properly trained by our very own Bristle. He would be appalled to hear you say any one of his trainees wasn't following through on his instruction."

Belle watched in fascination as the viscount, rather than being angered by his sister's reprimand, seemed to be highly amused.

"Always quick to point out my errors, aren't you, puss?" he asked gently. "You might be the one in need of correction. Surely your mother would tell you doing thusly in public is hardly the way to a gentleman's heart."

Lucretia grinned, clearly unrepentant. "I already know I'm firmly in your heart, so I needn't fear about that."

Again the viscount didn't argue with her on that point, but did point out her previous error. "You might note, sister dear, that I said the servants were unaccustomed to entertaining, not that they were uninformed on the subject. No insult to the resident servants nor to our Bristle was uttered or intended."

Lucretia laughed and shrugged. "Very well, carry on. But I don't think there was anything amiss."

"You haven't come out yet, though, so you might not be an expert on the subject," he pointed out.

"There could have been tea, but we were surprisingly perfectly fine," Lady Bathurst spoke up. "Thank you, my lord, for your solicitous treatment of us. You are being most genial."

Belle's eyebrows rose over her mother's sweet tone. It was the fakest thing she had ever witnessed and she wondered if everyone else in the room thought so. The youngsters, of course, wouldn't be aware, but surely their host would be. Again Belle was left to wonder what anyone was thinking. She longed for her bed. Not just any bed, and certainly not the one that had been offered her here at Lord Simmons' hunting lodge, but her comfortable, cozy spot at home, at Bathurst. Not really home any longer since her parents were so clearly eager to see her wed, but still she longed for it.

With a soft sigh, she pushed aside the unhelpful wish. She needed to find her place in her own future. Longing for what might be, or even what used to be, was unhelpful at best and hurtful at worst.

Chapter Six

Robert surveyed the room torn between laughter and dismay. He could hardly believe Bert and Lucy had turned up on his doorstep. And that he had Bathurst and the earl's family thrust upon him at the same time. What an odd situation to find himself in.

He watched in fascination as his sister preened under the female attention she was receiving even if it was from Lady Bathurst. Evidently, their mother hadn't changed her ways despite his most recent reprimand. The youngsters needed attention even if they were growing up so quickly. Or perhaps because they were growing up so quickly. But to Robert's mind, leaving them to the care of tutors and governesses was not sufficient for them to grow into well-developed adults.

And surely that should be every parent's intention.

Although, despite his various impressions, it would seem that Lady Isabelle had turned out to be a reasonably developed adult despite her odd parentage. He was glad to see she had recovered from her brief overindulgence. Perhaps her senses were still a little dulled as she seemed to find inordinate fascination in his brother and sister.

Robert was determined to keep his watchful eye on every person in that room. He still didn't know why his siblings had shown up unannounced. And, while he was sure he knew why Bathurst had shown up without warning, Robert couldn't be sure what they had planned for him next.

One thing that had surprised him, though, was how well Lady Bathurst had accepted the children.

Robert was briefly distracted by reminding himself that Lucy and Cuthbert were no longer children, as he had told Lady Isabelle, and they would not appreciate him thinking of them thusly.

His thoughts strayed back to Lady Bathurst's reception of them. Rather than the dismay he thought she would have felt over such a turn of events, she hadn't betrayed any negative feelings in the least. Robert had thought he detected a degree of calculation in her gaze, but he couldn't be certain what that might mean.

He would have to watch over all of them, one way or the other. He surveyed the room with varying degrees of interest before taking action.

There was an empty place next to Lady Isabelle. It was likely a calculated move, but Robert stepped forward to take the place despite having no intention of going along with her family's schemes. He still wasn't certain she was a willing participant in said scheme, but he would have to stay close to keep an eye on all of them anyway so there was nought else he could do.

“It was long and boring, but uneventful,” Robert heard Bert saying as he took a seat. It would seem everyone’s travels was still the topic of conversation.

“Will you do any fishing or hunting while you are visiting your brother?” Lady Isabelle turned the topic and asked Cuthbert.

Bert’s gaze flitted between Lucy and Robert before he returned it to earnestly stare into Lady Isabelle’s face. There was a problem Robert hadn’t anticipated. His little brother was starting an infatuation, Robert realised with a start and a smile he hurried to hide. It could end up a mess so he shouldn’t find it so immensely amusing.

“I am not certain we will be here long enough to do either of those,” Cuthbert finally answered with regret clear in his tone.

Lady Isabelle took it in stride. “If you *were* long enough, which would you prefer?”

“Fishing,” the boy answered promptly.

“A strapping young fellow like you?” Bathurst asked bracingly. “I would have expected you to say hunting.”

Cuthbert shrugged. “Seems to me that fishing takes much more patience and skill. And strikes me as being far less bloodthirsty.”

Lady Isabelle nodded approvingly, but her father shook his head.

“Nothing wrong with bloodthirst, my boy.”

“Father,” the young woman murmured, a reprimand in her tone that her father ignored with a chuckle.

Somehow Robert found Lady Isabelle more and more fascinating, which was odd considering he hadn't found his interest piqued by her much at all at the house party. Perhaps she improved upon continued acquaintance. It was also possible that she didn't show to advantage in the exalted company of such other fascinating people as the much-travelled Lady Constance or the high-spirited Miss Alcott.

Lady Isabelle had seemed to him to be a very pretty but empty-headed creature. Now, he wasn't so sure that he had been gracious to her at the house party.

Not to say that he had any interest in pursuing her despite her eligibility and even if she wasn't as silly as he had thought. No man wished for in-laws such as her parents. What else were they wont to do? While he was strangely curious about them, they did not appeal to him in the least and he could only imagine the sort of havoc they could create in their daughter's life for the rest her days.

And Robert had enough complications with his own mother and the youngsters to contend with. Still, he was duty-bound to keep an eye on his guests while they were in his home, especially now that Lucy and Bert had arrived. He couldn't very well leave his young siblings to fend for themselves with the vultures circling.

The mental picture he conjured amused him, and he caught Lady Isabelle watching him from the corner of her eye, seemingly taken aback by his smile. A frown formed to crease her forehead, but she kept her face averted.

What a contrary woman. Her attention was snagged by Lucy who wanted to discuss frocks, of all things. Lord Bathurst was growing bored.

"What have you stocked on your land for hunting?"

"I haven't gone to the trouble of stocking it, my lord. But it is naturally supplied with stag and boar as well as all manner of birds."

"Ah, you enjoy a challenge, then, do you, my boy?"

Rather than take offence, Robert was amused by the avuncular address. He hadn't felt like a boy for at least a decade, and even before that, no one had called him such since he had been in short pants.

"Father." The whispered word told Robert even more about Lady Isabelle. She wanted to protest her father's behaviour but didn't quite bring herself to do so aloud. He wondered at the relationship between the young lady and her parents. Was she frightened of them? Or merely respectful?

Robert couldn't picture the jovial Lord Bathurst mistreating anyone aside from perhaps the mistreatment of neglect as he pursued his own interests. And, of course, if the girl wasn't in agreement with her parents' scheme, forcing her into it was an abuse in itself. Robert's protective instincts were twitching, but there was nothing he could do. He had his own concerns and responsibilities, he reminded himself with a frown as he wondered anew why his brother and sister had shown up, and when he could return to the messages on his desk.

Aside from the nearly unvoiced protest, Lady Isabelle turned her attention back to Lucy and appeared to ignore the rest of the company.

"I cannot wait to shop on Bond Street," Lucy declared with dramatic glee.

"What makes you so eager to give them your patronage?" Isabelle inquired gently.

"They have to be so much better than the stores in our village."

"Have you ever been to Town?" the young lady asked.

"Of course, but Mother wouldn't allow me to go about much so it was hardly worth the drive."

"What has changed that you are so eager to go now? Are you of age?"

Robert wasn't sure if she was trying to hide the surprise in her voice, but she hadn't quite managed it. Or perhaps she had intentionally allowed it to be heard in order to plant seeds of doubt in his sister's mind. Not that Robert expected the young girl to be able to catch something so subtle. But he caught it. Or perhaps that was the plan all along.

How devious was the young lady?

Lucy harumphed much as Robert had expected her to over such a question. "No, I'm not of age. No one will agree to allow me to debut, least of all Robert here," the girl complained with a pout. Robert was surprised to hear a tinkle of laughter coming from Lady Isabelle.

"Making your debut is not the pure delight you think it's going to be, let me assure you. It is best that you not try to force yourself into it any sooner than your family think is timely."

"But why?" Lucy nearly wailed although she managed to keep the volume down. Robert supposed he ought to consider it a whine instead of a wail. He wanted to continue listening to Lady Isabelle's reasoning but was torn between listening to that conversation and the one Bathurst was having with Cuthbert.

Robert's young brother was also his heir until he could bring himself to wed and have children of his own so he took particular interest in the boy's upbringing. Since Bert was so much younger, Robert often felt as though he couldn't relate to the boy's thinking. Cuthbert had been still in short pants when their father had died and so had received far less of that man's influence. Robert loved his mother, of course, but didn't agree with most of her ideas about childrearing without her husband. Robert found himself regularly interfering with the children. Of course, he didn't think it was interference, but that was what his mother considered it. Robert's teeth gritted together at the memory of their last conversation on the matter.

"If you would wed and had children of your own, I might consider your opinion valid, Robbie, but since you haven't seen to that duty, you have no grounds upon which to judge me."

How she managed to dig at him on two separate topics in one sentence, was a skill Robert had no wish to develop. But she was a professional at it.

She had also wished to remarry.

Robert nearly shuddered. He hated having to deal with a stepfather at his ripe age of nearly thirty. His mother's judgement had never been the best. She never accepted the consequences of her actions. At times, when dealing with his mother, Robert was reminded of his siblings—they all needed to grow up. But with Lucy and Bert, there was still hope—not so much his mother.

"I cannot in good conscience carry on with my life until I feel my responsibilities to your father are completed. Your estate has to be secured before I can fully move on."

"My estate is just fine, Mother. You wished to wed, that is your affair and really has little to no effect upon anything I do, as you should understand, since you've already done as you wished. But can you truly say your duty to Father is complete with the children still young?"

"If you have an heir of your own, other than Cuthbert, he isn't part of your concern and you needn't keep sticking your oar into my dealings with the children."

Robert had argued strenuously on that subject. Little did his mother realise that her offer to remove the children from his influence was going to have the opposite effect upon his desire to wed. He couldn't allow her to take them off and be raised completely by someone else. Before she'd made her choice, he'd had little confidence in her judgement to choose a suitable second husband for herself. She hadn't, in fact, done a terrible job of it, but he would never allow her to take Cuthbert and Lucy away from him for any length of time.

It would seem his sister was of the same mind as him if their appearance on his doorstep today was any indication. But he couldn't allow Lucy to think of making her debut at her age, either. He himself was in no rush to wed. He couldn't countenance her rush to the altar just to get away from their mother's mercurial moods.

His thoughts returned to the room. It would seem Cuthbert and Bathurst were merely discussing which fish were most common to find on his properties. To Robert's surprise, Lady Bathurst was listening with what appeared to be genuine interest. There was no trouble there for the moment.

"Until you have enough understanding of people, it is better that you not enter Society," Lady Isabelle was trying to explain to Lucy.

"But how am I to understand people if I never meet any?" Lucy argued, bringing another laugh to the lady at her side.

"You do ask a good question," she countered as her eyes travelled to enmesh with Robert's gaze. Robert's breath caught in his throat for a moment, and he felt an almost maidenly shiver of attraction, but she turned her attention back to his sister without noticing, or so he hoped, at least.

"You would benefit from meeting people and getting a little bronze before officially making your debut. But surely that is still at least a couple years out. You are far from the shelf, my dear girl."

Lucy shrugged, appearing defiant and mutinous. "I don't much care for living with Mama and her husband," she said quietly despite the expression on her face telling them she wanted to rant on the topic.

"I'm sorry," Lady Isabelle answered quietly as she again glanced in his direction. "Perhaps your brother..." she trailed off as though she didn't want to commit him to anything.

"Mama says I cannot live with a bachelor," Lucy declared, making the other lady bite back laughter that came out almost as a snort.

"So did you come here to convince him to wed?" Lady Isabelle asked, clearly torn between laughter and disapproval.

"No, I just don't care what Mama says anymore. And I brought Bert, so surely there is nothing scandalous about it."

Lady Isabelle smiled gently, and Robert suspected that she sighed. She leaned closer to his sister so he couldn't hear everything she said, but he caught the gist of it.

He heard her explain that it wasn't his unwed state that was the scandalous part; it was the sort of activities a bachelor might become involved in that a young girl shouldn't be exposed to. Lucy's eyes were wide and round as she tried to fathom what the other woman was saying. The way the young girl looked at Lady Isabelle was akin to hero worship, and again, Robert cursed the coincidence that had them all at his house at the same time. It wouldn't do for Lucy to transfer all her pent-up adoration to a woman she might never see again. Well, he supposed she would eventually if Lady Isabelle wed with a titled gentleman. She would surely be around Town during the Season, and their paths would cross when Lucy finally took her place in Society. But it was unlikely they were to become or remain friends.

Robert's head began to ache along with his heart. He felt for his brother and sister. Their mother's sudden marriage had precipitated discomfort for all of them. While their father had been gone so long that the youngsters barely remembered him, they had been raised to respect his memory. That their mother would so suddenly marry was confusing for them. Robert still wasn't sure why she had rushed so madly into a union after professing her determination to savour being a widow ever since she gained that status.

Not to say that Robert wished his mother to be unhappy. But he didn't see that her sudden marriage had brought immense happiness with it. His mother was just as nagging and shrill as she had ever been, as far as he could tell. She also was still just as manipulative as she had ever been. Now she just brought further intensity to what she considered her role. It seemed to Robert as though his mother's recent marriage made her all the more determined to rid herself of what she saw as her final responsibilities toward her first husband. If Robert would wed, then he could take the other children off her hands and she would be free to wallow in being the new Countess Norton. Her duty would be concluded. And it was doubtful the earl expected children from her since she was well into her forties, not that she would admit to such advanced age. But his years of life gave hers away, surely.

Again, Robert acknowledged that he would have to do as she insisted no matter how much the thought palled him. His glance shifted back toward the picture Lady Isabelle presented with her head bowed next to Lucy's, but he nearly shook his own head in denial of the errant thought.

He was not going to wed someone just because his mother insisted. And he certainly wasn't going to wed with someone scheming to entrap him. He could not reward such deviant behaviour. Not to say that he was such a treat, Robert reminded himself. But it was what her parents so clearly wanted even if she wasn't in league with them. He couldn't be forced. He refused to be forced.

But his mother's machinations had often worked on his father, despite that man's wisdom and experience. His great love for his wife had been an easy thing for the woman to manipulate. Robert loved his mother but obviously not in the same way his father had. He hoped that would be enough to keep him safe from her schemes. But he wasn't certain it would.

Lucy and Bert's presence there might be just one more of her tactics. Or it might be their plea for help. Or possibly, both options were true.

And even if it was a scheme of his mother's, if his siblings needed him, he would do what needed to be done.

This sort of reasoning was probably exactly what got his father in trouble. But it had also resulted in his siblings, so Robert couldn't be completely sorry for it.

But one manipulative woman in his life was more than enough for any man.

Chapter Seven

Isabelle did her very best to ignore Lord Simmons, but his glowering presence made that difficult. The man was far too handsome for his own good and for her peace of mind. She ignored how he made her feel, at least if they were the warm sort of feelings. If he made her angry, she would happily fan the flames of that sort of feeling.

But she was feeling far too fatigued for anger at the moment. And contrarily, the other type of feeling was trying to overtake the boundaries she had set up. Belle was determined to disregard such thoughts.

Miss Lucretia was a delight. Belle had forgotten how much she had wished for a younger sibling. Sitting and chatting with the girl made her feel old and wise despite her relative few years. It made her start to think a little more favourably about wedding. Perhaps having children would fill that desire.

She flickered a glance toward her unwilling host. Perhaps she ought to consider matching with a gentleman with younger siblings. Certainly not

Lord Simmons despite how appealing his young brother and sister might be. But someone with similar circumstances.

Isabelle fell silent as she pondered which gentlemen she had met who might allow her to take a hand with his wards.

"You appear to be plotting."

The deep voice coming from behind her almost made her squeak from surprise. She had been so lost in thought that she hadn't noticed that the other occupants of the room had moved about. Heat flushed her face.

"I was wool gathering; my apologies, it has been a long day," she stammered out in confusion, further surprised by his sudden laughter.

"That much was evident, my dear, but nothing you need apologise for. It has been a long day for all of us. You are allowed to be tired."

The heat in her face didn't abate. A debutante ought to always appear as fresh as a daisy, she reminded herself with a sigh.

"Don't pucker up. I assure you, no one took the least offence. Well, maybe my sister as you became far less interesting."

Despite her intention to ignore the handsome man, she couldn't help but laugh over his words.

"I'm sure I have been a total bore. How appallingly remiss of me. Where has the dear girl gone off to?"

"I promise, you weren't wool gathering for more than ten minutes. Just enough time for her to determine that she ought to show your mother around."

"Oh dear," Belle commented, wondering what her mother might be getting up to now.

"Don't let it worry you. My sister isn't as easily lead as she might make you think."

Isabelle wasn't completely sure what he meant by the cryptic comment, but she wasn't about to ask him for fear it would be something she would feel obligated to take exception to out of loyalty to her mother. She offered him a weak smile.

"But I must admit that I am consumed with curiosity as to what could have so absorbed you that you didn't notice."

Heat again flooded through her, and Isabelle wondered if she was about to catch fire, so hot were her cheeks. And she could never admit to the man that she had been wondering which available gentlemen had youngsters in their household. It was unlikely to be well-received from the man who already appeared to have suspicions of his uninvited guests. She wasn't very good at making up excuses, but she would do her best.

"As you said, travel fatigued me. I just allowed my mind to wander."

"You appeared most absorbed," he commented.

Belle shrugged. What was she supposed to say to that?

"As I said, my lord, my sincerest apologies." She sounded testy even to her own ears, but she couldn't find it within herself to care.

"And as I said, you needn't apologise," he countered, and Belle could hear laughter in his voice which she tried hard not to bristle over. "In fact, I must owe you an apology for persisting in my curiosity."

Just like that, Belle was disarmed. She struggled against it. She had no interest in liking the gentleman. The situation her parents had thrust upon her aside, she had no intention of allowing her heart to become entangled with a gentleman who had decided against her. And she was never going to pursue a man no matter what her parents thought. To her mind, it was a recipe for disaster. Just look at her sister. Augusta had pursued her husband, fully expecting a love match, but it would appear now that they could barely tolerate one another.

No, Belle was determined that her future husband would come to her. He had to value her above all else. She didn't expect a love match, even if they were becoming more common amongst some of her acquaintances. Just look at the three betrothals they had witnessed during the house party. All seemed to be varying degrees of intense emotion involved. That was lovely and all, but Belle wasn't going to hold out for the same for herself. But she *did* expect the gentleman to recognise her value. It could even be her dowry he valued, or her familial connections, or some other thing she couldn't think of with her brain turned to fatigued mush at the moment. But any gentleman she would commit herself to had to be the one to choose her. She would never accept that he felt he had settled for her. That his defences had been worn down by her pursuit. Or in this case, her parents' pursuit.

For the rest of their days, she would have to continue to pursue him in such a case. Belle had no interest in such a circumstance, thank you very much.

And she cared very little how un-dutiful that made her. Was it not her parents' duty to ensure she experienced at least a modicum of happiness or at least comfort for the rest of her life? And whichever gentleman she eventually matched with would have to be the father of her children. She refused to saddle said non-existent future children with a disinterested father.

Not to say that a gentleman who wasn't interested in his wife would be disinterested in his children, but from what she could see of Lord Simmons, he hadn't taken a very elaborate interest in his brother and sister who had quite literally turned up on his doorstep.

Of course, Belle argued to herself, those very same youngsters had felt comfortable showing up, so there must be some sort of familial comfort between them.

No, she reminded herself, Lord Simmons was absolutely not for her. She wouldn't even consider him. It mattered little if he was now watching her with curious interest. It was too late. There had been nearly a fortnight in which he could have taken an interest in her.

Belle made good on her thoughts, gaining her feet and announcing to the room that she would seek her bed.

"Oh dear, already?" Both Miss Lucy and Lady Bathurst seemed disappointed to see her leave just as they were returning to the room. For a moment, Belle's heart was warmed, but she implored herself to ignore the sensation. She needed sleep to fortify her resistance to her parents' schemes the next day.

But then she wondered if there were enough bedchambers in his lordship's lodge to house all of his sudden guests. It was a lovely place, but she hadn't received the impression that it was overly large. Certainly nothing like Everleigh, where they had been spending the last several days, the Earl of Everleigh's country seat. Of course, nearly nowhere was as large as that, she thought with a shake of her silly head. Bathurst was a comfortable size and would no doubt fit into one wing of the massive edifice.

Still, she wondered if she ought to ensure Lucretia was looked after or if she would need to share Belle's room.

A quick glance around the room reminded her that Lord Simmons had sufficient staff despite his claim that they were unused to entertaining. She could be sure they had thought of all the arrangements. It would have been dealt with by now, and it was not her problem in any case. As their host, Lord Simmons would deal with whatever needed dealing.

Without further mental wrangling and with few more words, Belle had made her escape from the suddenly overwhelming situation.

She couldn't have even explained it if she were asked, why she was suddenly so desperate to quit the room. She had never been one to run away from awkward or uncomfortable situations.

Of course, she had never found herself in anything quite like these particular circumstances.

As far as she knew, her parents had never schemed to match up any of their other offspring. Perhaps, Belle thought, she ought to write to her oldest brother. As the heir, it was likely he could intervene on her behalf. But he had never professed much interest in her affairs before. Belle was unsure if she could count on him.

She was sure she could count on herself and that was all that mattered.

~~~~

The next day saw an improvement in at least her viewpoint if not the entire situation. Lord Simmons' servants and the Bathurst coachman, along with the local smithy, were able to arrange for a repair of their carriage, but Lord Bathurst claimed he wasn't comfortable relying upon the repair all the way to London so it was soon agreed that the entire party would travel together in two carriages. The ladies would travel together in one while Lord Bathurst would follow them in the repaired carriage. Lord Simmons and Cuthbert
~~~~

would alternate between riding and sitting with the earl or the ladies depending on their moods.

They amused themselves as best they could for the day at Lord Simmons' hunting lodge and would set out early on the third day.

The day was fine and the location ideal, if one had intended to spend a day doing not much of anything at all. Belle had not done so which made it frustrating for her. She felt squashed between her mother's insistence that she get Lord Simmons on a matrimonial hook and the same gentleman's resistance to any such thing.

Of course, he was everything polite whenever they encountered one another, but Belle felt he was taking her on sufferance—that it was mere social nicety that had him even being polite, as though he wished he could show the lot of them the door and be done with them. Not that Belle could blame him, but it was certainly awkward.

He also seemed preoccupied. Perhaps he had business affairs he needed to see to, and their presence was a distraction he could ill afford, Belle thought as she stepped into his small library and found him poring over some papers.

He looked up and quickly shoved the papers under a book which struck Belle as odd. From this distance, she certainly couldn't read what was on the paper, even if she had meant to try. Her curiosity was piqued but she quelled the urge to question him.

"Can I be of assistance, my lady?" His question was perfectly polite but spoken in the coldest manner Belle had yet heard from him. She nearly quailed but couldn't bear to seem cowardly. She lifted her chin and was surprised to see his eyes flair. If she didn't think he thought her a ninny, she would have thought he found her attractive in that moment. Viscount Simmons was certainly a quandary. Not one she wished to unravel at her mother's command, but he certainly intrigued her despite her determined indifference.

"I was wondering if you might have a book I could borrow."

"Bored of strolling already?"

"Not bored, my lord, but I do long to read. It is one of my favourite pastimes, much to Mother's despair, and I haven't been able to indulge myself in days. When I realised your lodge contained a library, I thought you might understand. But if I'm disturbing you, I understand and I apologise." She was about to leave, but to her surprise he stood and beckoned her forward.

"It is me who must apologise. My thoughts were elsewhere, and my manners went begging. Come in. I don't have a great collection of books here, and I can't even be certain what might be on the shelves, but you're welcome to whatever you may find."

"Thank you. Please ignore my presence and carry on with whatever you were occupied with. I shan't disturb you, I promise."

The expression on his face indicated he didn't believe her, but he seated himself, and from the rustle of papers, Belle assumed he returned to what he was doing. It was a challenge for her to concentrate on the titles before her as her attention seemed to remain rooted in the gentleman at the desk, much to her consternation.

Why did the one gentleman least likely to want her for a wife turn out to be the only one who so interested her? She was the most ridiculous creature in the Kingdom. Finally, after a couple minutes, the allure of the unknown books pulled her attention firmly in, and she was caught up in exploring the viscount's eclectic selection. To such an extent that she didn't notice his approach.

"Have you found anything?" he asked, making her jump and nearly drop the book she had been skimming through.

"I think so. I thought I had read this one already, but now I don't think I have."

"It isn't likely you'll finish it today."

"No, but I shan't steal it, I promise."

His bark of laughter caused odd trembles in her belly. Combined with the jitters she was already experiencing from his nearness and the fact that it was only the two of them in the room, it was a heady sensation.

"Lady Isabelle."

They heard the faint call of his young sister searching for her new friend. Belle quickly stepped away from the viscount with a quick shake of her head that she followed up with a smile.

"Thank you, my lord. Again, I apologise for disturbing you at your work." She cast a curious glance toward his desk which was now completely clear of papers. Evidently, he was determined that she not see whatever had preoccupied him. "I may not even get a chance to read, but just perusing the titles felt like a little sojourn into unreality, which I needed. So I thank you again, and I'll bid you adieu."

With that, she veritably fled from his presence and went in search of Lucy even as she tried to remind her heart not to even think of setting its sights on Lord Simmons. Disaster for her lay in that direction.

True to her prediction, Belle didn't get a great deal of time to read, but the sojourn in the library had given her plenty to ponder as she strolled in the forest and dales with Lucy. She couldn't have told you what Lady Bathurst did to amuse herself while the younger ladies were absent. Belle surmised she was likely driving Lord Simmons' servants to distraction. She tried not to ponder overmuch on the man himself, but she had enjoyed her moments in his library.

The day was surprisingly pleasant for the various sources of discomfort.

Belle didn't consider herself particularly vain but she was beginning to think she would happily set fire to the gown she had spent all her time in for the past three days. It was heavy and made for travel, not leisurely house visits. It had served her well when she had gone for long rambles in the woods near the house, but sitting anywhere near a fire indoors made her wish she had at least a light change of clothing. The servants had all done their best to take care of her and her clothing, but she felt decidedly worse for wear by the time they set out for Town early the next morning.

Miss Lucretia was beside herself with delight, not even minding that she was forced to sit in the rear-facing seat.

"Mama always makes me sit here anyway, so I'm quite used to it, you know," she had advised Belle and Lady Bathurst as soon as they had settled in the carriage. "I can hardly credit that Robbie is letting us go with him. This is the most exciting development I could have hoped for. I expected him to allow us to visit him for a day or two and then he would send us packing back to Norton—that's where we live now, you know? Mama said we had to accompany her there when she married. She says Robbie might be our guardian, but she refuses to acknowledge what that means, and since he's never at home, we couldn't be left all on our own with the servants. I don't really see why not. It happened often enough before she wed, didn't it? And we're already older than we were then, so I don't see what the difference is. But now, Robbie says we can come with him, and we shall see how it goes. I really think it's because you all were there, don't you know? He probably didn't want to seem like an ogre in front of visitors. So I'm ever so grateful that your carriage had problems. And I know that sounds dreadful, but now, we have had a cozy visit, and I'm on my way to London, so it's the best thing ever."

Belle's eyes had widened as the girl had seemed to have an eruption of words. Isabelle couldn't even be certain that the girl had breathed in all that time. And then it took almost a full minute for the entire content of Lucy's words to process themselves in her mind. It must have been the same for her mother because she didn't stiffen and become starchy until the girl had grown silent.

"We certainly didn't break down for your benefit, my dear child," Lady Bathurst said in a frostier tone than she had been using with the girl.

"No, of course not, but it was a happy coincidence for me, wasn't it? And now we have all day to visit again together. Will you allow me to visit you while we're all in Town?" Lucy didn't seem the least bit repressed by Lady Bathurst's coolness. Belle bit her lip to control her amusement.

"Of course, as long as you don't wander about Town unaccompanied, though. We wouldn't want to bring scandal upon any of us."

Belle wasn't sure who to stare at—her mother for bringing up the thought of scandal or the young girl who was staring at Lady Bathurst with her mouth hanging open. To Belle's utter surprise, though, Miss Lucretia shut her mouth and quite deliberately looked down her nose at the countess.

"A Simmons would never court scandal," she said with great dignity. It took all of Isabelle's considerable determination not to burst into raucous laughter.

"No, of course you wouldn't," Belle quickly stepped into the conversation. "It is just so important that a lady protect her reputation that my mother felt the need to remind you of such."

She paused briefly before glancing at the girl pointedly. "You did show up to your brother's bachelor lodgings unannounced."

"As did you," the girl said, displaying far more shrewdness than Belle would have thought her capable.

"That may be true, but I had the protection of my parents."

"I suppose we could say that I had the protection of my guardian," Miss Lucretia countered.

Isabelle gave up on trying to hold off the laughter. While she did try to keep the volume down, she couldn't seem to prevent her mirth from expressing itself. In an effort to bring herself back under control, she turned her gaze to the window and nearly swallowed her tongue.

Lord Simmons was riding next to their carriage and was staring right at her. That sobered her quickly as mortification threatened to swamp her. Had he been there all along? Or did the sound of her laughter attract his attention? Did he think her a complete wanton?

She turned her head away pointedly, grateful that no one else in the carriage seemed to have noticed her discomfiture nor the viscount's scrutiny.

"Never mind all of that. Of course you'll have a care to your reputation. I daresay, you've been trained to do so from birth just as I have. Now tell me, what do you most hope to accomplish in Town besides shopping on Bond Street? And do you think to stay with your brother indefinitely?"

"Do you think he might allow it?" Suddenly, the girl's air of maturity fell away, and she was once more the eager child.

"I really couldn't say. But if he is, as you said, your guardian, I cannot imagine why he wouldn't." Belle ignored her mother's snort and the fact that it was evident her own parents were ready to see the back of her. It was most lowering.

"I do hope you are right, my lady. I would love that above all things. Even though Robbie can be strict and stuffy, he doesn't annoy us nearly as much as our mother's husband does. I think it safe to say Bert and I would be willing to promise any manner of good behaviour if only Robbie will agree to keep us."

"Won't your mother miss you?" Belle asked hesitantly.

"Oh, I doubt it. Only she won't want to admit as much, I would imagine," Lucy answered before her eyes widened. "I don't suppose I ought to have said that out loud, am I right, my lady?"

"Perhaps not. It would be best not to publicly criticise your mother."

"Oh, but we aren't public, are we? Aren't we friends?"

Entirely disarmed, Belle assured the girl of her continued friendship.

The youngster was delighted. "Thank you ever so much, my lady. I've always wanted a big sister. I'll happily make do with you."

Again Isabelle had to laugh, but she managed to keep it within bounds that time.

"And I often wished I wasn't the youngest, so I'll be happy to adopt you as my little sister." Belle again ignored her mother's evident disdain for the conversation as best she could but chose to steer the conversation into a better channel. "You didn't tell me what you have planned for your time in Town. If it turns out that your sojourn isn't as long as you'd like, you ought to set your priorities."

Lucy giggled like the young girl that she was. "I do hope to stay there forever, but I see the wisdom of your suggestion. And I cannot even be perfectly certain, aside from the shopping, what I'd most like to do. It's not likely I'll be invited for any grown-up sort of activities like balls or routs or even the theatre."

"Perhaps not, but it is likely there might be other children in town with their families. Perhaps his lordship could introduce you." Belle winced over her mistaken use of the word children but was relieved that the girl didn't seem to take offence.

While the young girl prattled on about all she was excited about seeing in Town, Belle allowed her mind to wander along with her gaze. The carriage they were in was quite exquisite. It was clear the viscount was not a nipfarthing. It appeared the carriage had either been very recently reupholstered or it was never used. And the springs were exceptionally well mounted. Despite her family's previously well-to-do status, any carriage she had ever ridden in had been far more bouncy and rough over the poorly tended roads between home and Town.

And his sister's clothes. She was very well dressed for such a youngster. Isabelle hadn't been released from extremely boring and mundane serges that could be considered almost a uniform, much like the servants wore, until she was nearly ready to make her debut. Of course, Belle also didn't go anywhere or see anyone when she was a youngster, so she supposed it hadn't really mattered what she wore, but it was clear to her that either Lord Simmons or his mother's new husband was generous with the girl's clothing allowance.

Curiosity gripped her as to who was the one filling her clothes cupboard. Her gaze sought him out, but the viscount was no longer riding postillion.

Chapter Eight

Robert was thinking very colourful language as he rode next to his brother. How had he gotten himself into this predicament? How had he gone from comfortably solo to escorting the clearly conniving Lord Bathurst's trio as well as his young brother and sister?

It would be farcical if it wasn't, in all reality, working out reasonably well. It had been a recipe for near disaster, but that had not come to fruition, much to Rob's relief.

But now what was he to do?

He wasn't terribly surprised to have received his siblings. Lucy had been writing him more and more urgent letters for weeks now, expressing how very unhappy they were in their mother's new home. Robert hadn't been happy about their removal to Norton, but he had not thought it fitting to remove them from their mother at the time. Now, they had taken the matter into their own hands. Or perhaps their mother had put them up to it.

And that was the root of his dilemma.

Was he to marry to provide a female influence for the children? Or was that exactly what his mother was trying to pressure him into doing?

If it wasn't for his mother's manipulations, he would be eager to find himself wed and settled to provide a suitable environment for Lucy and Bert. But if it was their mother scheming, he wanted to send them all packing. The tricks and schemes his mother had enjoyed plying had played havoc with Robert's childhood. For that reason, he was particularly averse to allowing any more to touch his life.

Which was why he needed to strive for rational thought. Whether it was their mother's schemes or not, if his brother and sister were truly unhappy with their mother's new situation, he would have no other choice but to take them in. Perhaps he should have planned for that all along. It had been his inclination, but their mother had convinced him that she could not be separated from her children, and despite his own complicated relationship with her, he had agreed that children needed their mother. He had lacked his mother when he was their age, and he wouldn't wish that on the youngsters. When they had been in the nursery, there was little he could do for them anyway. But they were growing up faster than he could note, and he needed to stick his oar into their affairs immediately.

His own feelings would have to be left out of the matter.

Watching Lucy become so animated under the questionable attentions of Lady Bathurst and her daughter had proven the girl needed an interested female in her life. Robert had contemplated falling into the Bathursts' scheme for the briefest moment, especially when he had heard Lady Isabelle's surprised laughter. It had sounded so joyful and carefree. Rob had warmed to it immediately.

But then he had called himself to account. She was barely more than a girl herself. She was not what he needed even if she weren't a scheming hussy. But he would redouble his efforts during the rest of this Season.

How he was to accomplish that while also watching over his siblings and taking his responsibilities within the House of Lords, as well as the investigation he was supposed to be undertaking, might currently be a mystery for him but he had every confidence he would be able to figure it out. With a nod, Robert resolved that he would be wed before the Season ended. Then he could take his new wife and the youngsters home to his estate for the summer, and they could all settle in.

It was just too bad he hadn't found success at the house party. Three betrothals and none of them his. Robert wasn't one to berate himself for the past, but surely he hadn't been taking the matter seriously enough. He knew his efforts had been half-hearted at best at Everleigh. He had been inclined to court the very suitable Miss Alcott, but she had not turned out to be the suitable and serious young woman he had thought her. It had been a surprise to everyone when she had chosen to marry the most adventurous of Lord Everleigh's five sons.

Never mind that, Robert admonished himself. *Think through who else would be suitable from the available ladies that Season.* Surely he could find one for himself.

But his dilemma was that all the suitably mature and matronly women available didn't appeal to him for a lifelong partner. The ones he thought suitable to guide his sister didn't seem like ones he would enjoy meeting across his breakfast table every morning for the rest of his days.

With a shrug, Robert reminded himself that duty was duty, and he didn't much care about breakfast anyway. He had a few weeks ahead of him to find the right compromise. Failure to do so was not an option.

When another quickly stifled sweet tinkle of laughter came from his carriage, Robert moved farther away. Growing attracted to Lady Isabelle was surely not going to help his determination to wed appropriately.

After a brief stop for luncheon at an inn halfway between his lodge and Town, it was late afternoon when they finally pulled up in front of the Bathurst London townhouse. Lord Bathurst climbed out quickly, looking surly, before his coachman pulled around to the mews, but then they were left waiting when no one emerged from his own carriage. Finally, Robert stepped forward to where a servant had already let down the steps and was waiting at the open door.

The ladies were still deep in conversation. Lucy's serious, attentive face was focused intently on whatever Lady Isabelle was saying. Robert didn't much appreciate the satisfied expression upon Lady Bathurst's face. It reminded him of his own mother whenever she had managed to maneuver him into doing exactly what she wanted.

Robert wanted to snatch his sister out of the carriage and ensure she had nothing further to do with either of its other occupants. But since it was his own carriage, he couldn't rightly do that.

He cleared his throat to gain their attention. Lady Isabelle broke off what she was saying immediately and cast an expression of regret at him.

"My apologies, my lord. You would think we would have gotten it all said before we arrived, wouldn't you?" She was clearly embarrassed and surprised by her own tardy behaviour. Robert refused to be charmed. He put his hand out, and Lady Bathurst grasped it, allowing him to help her down first.

When Robert turned back to the occupants of the carriage, it was clear Lady Isabelle didn't particularly want to accept his assistance. Perversely, this made Robert all the more determined to give it. He kept a pleasant smile in place and his hand outstretched.

He wasn't prepared for the sparks that he felt when she reluctantly placed her small hand into his large one. Hers was certainly not the same as his sister's hand. He had never experienced such a sensation despite the myriad hands he had undoubtedly touched.

It took effort, but he managed not to snatch his hand away. He was inordinately proud of himself for that accomplishment despite how foolish it felt. As a gentleman, not insulting a lady should be the norm, not requiring effort.

The way her eyes fluttered up to meet his gaze and then quickly away like a nervous little bird told him Lady Isabelle was not as immune to his proximity as she would have him believe with her usually cool exterior. The flush that tinged her cheeks a becoming rose also indicated her agitation. Robert liked it but tried very hard not to be affected by her.

"Thank you for escorting us home, my lord. I know it wasn't what you had planned with your time."

It wasn't, but how else was a gentleman to respond?

"It was my pleasure, my lady. And my sister, at the very least, was delighted with the turn of events."

Her expression told him he had probably insulted her slightly. A quick review of his words made him almost wince, but he chose to ignore the gaff. He wasn't going to mince his words or apologise for every possible perceived slight. If she was going to go about in Society, she would need to be ready for rudeness wherever she went.

"Your sister is a delight; it was our pleasure entirely to have her company for the journey," Lady

Isabelle said quietly as she finally stepped out of the carriage and away from him. “I trust the short journey that remains for you will be uneventful.”

“Good day, my lady.” Robert bowed to Isabelle and then again to Lady Bathurst before he swung back up onto the back of his horse while the servants folded the stairs back up and shut the door of the carriage.

“Goodbye,” Lucy called, waving madly from the window she had opened. “I will call as soon as I am able.”

Robert gritted his teeth. It would seem he wouldn’t be rid of the Bathurst trio anytime soon if his sister had any say in the matter.

They quickly made their way to his townhouse. The mess in his foyer told him his sister had already arranged for her and her brother’s belongings to be transferred to Town.

“We haven’t even discussed your circumstances, and yet, I see evidence that you have taken up residence.”

His sister had the grace to blush, but Cuthbert launched into speech. “Lucy said, really, this is our home, too, Robbie. Surely you won’t mind. I swear to you we’ll stay out of your way, and you needn’t pay us any mind in the least.”

“You cannot seriously think I would allow you to take up residence with me and then simply ignore the pair of you,” Robert countered before he glanced around at the gathered servants staring agog. “Never mind, let us repair to my library and discuss this in detail.”

After directing the servants to arrange for the baggage and have tea served in his library, Rob walked in front of his brother and sister into his most private room. He rarely saw people in his library. He chose to conduct any business he needed to do either in an office at the House of Lords or at Whites. So it felt meaningful to speak with the youngsters there. At least to him. They no doubt had no idea of its significance. Robert sighed. It was time that it be rectified. Past time, in all actuality.

"Did anything particularly untoward happen to precipitate your choice to remove from your mother's presence?"

To his relief, Lucy grinned. "She's your mother, too, Robbie, even if you don't always like her." There was a pause as Lucy and Bert exchanged a glance Robert couldn't interpret. "Nothing in particular or one specific thing. It just became unbearable. The earl doesn't want us there, and that's his right, in my opinion. I cannot say what sort of promises Mother might have made him when they agreed to wed, but it was evident from the beginning that he hadn't expected us to be a part of their arrangement."

"Well, surely the fool knew she had children," Robert couldn't help interjecting.

Lucy just shrugged. "You would think so. But who knows? I don't think he lacks intellect. But he has made no secret of his displeasure at our continued presence."

"And you didn't seek protection at school?"

"Since I've never gone, I thought it a bit late for me to try it now," Lucy began. "And Bert didn't want to leave me to fend for myself."

"School isn't so great, anyway," Cuthbert stated with such determination that Rob was certain his brother was only saying that to spare his sister's feelings. Robert's resolve solidified. He didn't relish the thought of taking on full responsibility for the half-grown children, but there was no other choice. They *were* his responsibility, and he needed to live up to it. And besides his natural familial affection for them, he quite liked them most of the time, even if they were going to complicate his life considerably.

"I ought to have asked this as soon as you turned up on my doorstep, but I will admit to having been thoroughly distracted by various other matters. Does Mother know where you are?"

The youngsters exchanged another glance that made Robert suddenly nervous.

"If you've left her to wonder and worry about you, I shan't think at all highly of either of you. You might have your reasons for not wishing to live with her, but you owe her the respect of not leaving her to fret."

"We would never do that, Robbie; you ought to know us better than that. I doubt she would have noticed our absence, though, since we've only been gone a couple of days. But yes, we left a note telling her of our plans."

"A note," Robert repeated dully. "Did you truly consider that sufficient?"

"Well, you *are* our guardian," Lucy declared with a defiant tone before she hung her head. "It might not have been perfectly sufficient, Robbie, but at least we didn't just run away into the night. We did inform her of our whereabouts. And I didn't just leave it on my pillow. We left it with the butler to give to her when she arose. And the servants all knew, so it wasn't the least bit havey-cavey. As you know, I even brought my maid."

"I know, my dear, and I'm sorry for raking you over the coals, but I might have been tempted to run off into the night if I were you, so I suppose I spoke out of turn." He grinned at his siblings before adding, "I will have a courier take a note confirming that I have you and that I will be taking over your care from here on out. You must prepare yourselves for some protest from her, even if you think she doesn't mean it. She won't want her friends to think she hasn't taken proper care of you."

"Well, she hasn't," Bert muttered. "Are you certain you shan't mind taking us on?"

"Not in the least. In fact, I should have thought of it before now. I just didn't realise that the time was carrying on so and you'd nearly grown before I realised you were no longer in nappies."

Cuthbert grinned and shook his head.

"First things first, though. What did you do with your tutor?"

"Mother's husband tossed him out, so I didn't do anything with him."

Robert stared at his brother and wondered if that was the full story.

"So you haven't been studying?"

"I've been studying, just not having any instruction. The rector gave me a few lessons now and again, but nothing formal."

"When did this take place?" Robert tried to keep his fury out of his voice, but he must not have been completely successful if the expressions on his siblings' faces were anything to go by as they again exchanged one of their silent conversations in front of him.

"A month ago."

"And you're just telling me about it now?"

Cuthbert shrugged. "I was expecting they'd get me another one, but that didn't happen."

"That was just one more reason why we came to you, Robbie," Lucy explained. "You know Bert is brilliant and ought to be in school. It's hard to believe, but he enjoys filling his head with books."

Robert laughed. "We should all do at least a little bit of that, Luce."

Lucy shrugged and laughed. "I'm in an awkward position, to be honest. Rather a little old for a nursery maid and not overly used to having a governess but not quite grown either," she said, sounding incredibly mature to her older brother despite only achieving her fourteenth summer. "I'd be happy to read or study whatever you think right, though, if that would make you feel better."

Robert couldn't help but laugh. "I don't know if it would exactly make me feel better, but it would certainly be appropriate. Not that I have the firmest of understanding what sort of education a young lady ought to have. Mother should have seen to it more particularly than she has done." He sighed, raking a hand through his hair. He paused in thought, staring at her for a moment. "Do you have languages and drawing and needlework and some sort of an instrument?"

"I'm sadly rather rudimentary at all of those things," Lucy admitted without much sadness reflecting in her tone.

"Well, that's a good place to start. Most of those things merely require practice, if you have a start to them. So we needn't hire you a tutor unless you feel you want to learn even more. But I will have to look into what else you need to know." He stared at his sister. "I swear I'm not trying to get rid of you, but it might be best if we found a school for you to attend for a spell."

"I'll think on it," Lucy promised, but Robert didn't hold out much hope of her doing so. He determined to ask amongst the ladies of his acquaintance what he ought to do with her. Not that he really knew whom he could ask. A picture of Lady Isabelle flashed before his eyes. She seemed to be well-versed in all the various things a young lady ought to know. *But was she in any position to advise him?* And he couldn't trust her in the first place, even if she were, he reminded himself as he closed his mind to the attraction he struggled against in her presence.

Chapter Nine

"You again didn't avail yourself of the perfect opportunity, foolish girl."

Lady Bathurst's tone wasn't as hurtful as the words she used so Isabelle didn't think her mother was truly angry with her, but still, she sighed. She had been doing her best to ignore her parents' odd insistence that she entrap the viscount, but she was done with that strategy.

"I cannot understand your intent, Mother. Why are you so desperate to have me off your hands?"

Lady Bathurst stared, surprised by her daughter's sudden display of backbone.

"It is time, Isabelle. You are out of the schoolroom. Your father and I wish to get on with the rest of our lives, with no more children to see to."

Belle frowned. "I didn't realise my presence was such a burden."

Lady Bathurst didn't recognise the sarcasm. "I wouldn't use the word burden, my dear. I'm just tired of being responsible for you."

Isabelle lifted her chin. "I can absolve you of the responsibility without needing to entrap a husband."

"Don't be even more foolish than usual, Isabelle. You cannot absolve me. I am responsible for you until you wed."

Isabelle sighed anew. She couldn't really argue with her mother's logic. It was just so very unexpected. She never would have foreseen that she would be rushed into marriage. They were far from destitute. She had actually thought to take an extra year before even making her debut and had only agreed to do so now as a sort of lark, thinking she could enjoy it and be serious later. Trepidation filled her, and she felt even more alone than usual.

How was she to make such a big decision when her so-called advisors had far different motivations than she thought important? That was to say, were her parents pushing her toward Viscount Simmons because they thought him a good match for her or because he was available and eligible?

It didn't matter, despite her mother's apparent fatigue with her position, Belle wasn't going to wed with someone who would later consider her a burden. Already her parents evidently thought her one. She had no intention of carrying on this experience for the rest of her days.

"Perhaps we could hire a companion to escort me and it needn't fall to you," Belle suggested as gently as she could.

"That would look highly irregular," Lady Bathurst countered.

"So you don't want to be responsible for me anymore, but you don't want anyone to know that's how you feel; is that what you are telling me?"

"Don't make it sound so dreadful, Isabelle," Lady Bathurst commanded with a frown. "It isn't really unusual for a mother to expect her daughter to wed in her first Season. I daresay, most mothers have that intention. It's usually rather competitive amongst the mothers and matrons of the *ton.*"

"That may well be, but you have never been one of those matrons," Belle pointed out.

"Things change, Isabelle. It is time for you to grow up and accept that."

Belle was surprised by the scratch of tears threatening behind her eyes. She was not usually a weeper. Perhaps she was merely tired from the days of travel. Of course, being disappointed by her mother's attitude and words was natural, but as she said, the situation wasn't excessively unusual. If only she had been given a little warning, she might have been able to enter into the spirit of the matter. Now she only felt wrong-footed and behind the times.

How was she to find her match so suddenly with the Season nearing its conclusion? They never should have accepted the invitation to the Everleigh house party. She should have been in Town finding her match.

But there had been thought that she might make a match at the party. And she hadn't realised her parents were in earnest about hurrying her to the altar. So she refused to castigate herself on the subject.

What she needed was a plan.

Without further conversation and barely even a curtsy, Belle left her mother in the foyer. Since the carriage carrying their trunks and boxes had arrived days ago, Belle was confident she was not needed. She hurried up to her bedchamber.

Belle was relieved to find her maid waiting for her. She wanted nothing more than to shred the gown she had been wearing for the last three days, but she knew that was a ridiculous thought. All it really needed was some treatment in the laundry and for her not to see it for a while.

"Welcome home, my lady. I'm ever so glad to see you. I've been that worried about you."

The maid was bobbing curtsies as she spoke, but Belle hurried forward and pulled the other woman into a quick but warm embrace.

"I've missed you, Ellen. I was desperate for you these last days. And not just because you are so much better at doing my hair than I am."

Ellen laughed as had been Isabelle's intention, but she quickly stepped away after returning her mistress' warm squeeze.

"Should I draw you a bath, my lady?"

They hadn't been travelling for very long, and since her mother was so eager to see her wed, Belle supposed she couldn't cry off from whichever entertainments they were promised to that evening.

"That would be most enjoyable, thank you," Belle responded with a smile as her maid helped her out of her gown before hurrying from the room to arrange for the water to be boiled and brought.

In the meantime, Belle was determined to figure out a plan. In her dressing gown, she settled behind the small desk in her chamber and pulled a sheet of paper towards herself. It took her a while to get her thoughts in order, but she was soon jotting down a list of the eligible gentlemen she could consider. While she very much wanted to understand what was behind her parents' sudden wish to see the back of her, it didn't really change the fact that she needed to wed eventually. She felt the urge to resist, but that was likely futile. She might as well make the most of finding her own idea of a suitable match rather than just accepting her parents' choice.

Her pencil spent more time tapping her chin than it did scratching across her paper, but by the time her maid called her to the bath, Isabelle had assembled a small list of possibilities.

"You appeared to be hard at work, my lady. Is there something I ought to be helping you with?" The maid asked the question even as she was pouring water over her mistress.

"Thank you, Ellen, but I don't think there is, in this instance, unfortunately."

"You do seem troubled, though. Were you dreadfully put out by your difficulties on the way home?"

Belle sighed, grateful to have someone who was thinking about her feelings.

"I am troubled, in truth of fact, and it only sort of ties in with the troubles we had." Belle couldn't very well tell her maid she suspected her parents had sabotaged their own carriage, but she could admit she was under more pressure to wed than expected. "I hadn't truly thought to wed this Season, despite my coming to Town and making my debut."

"I don't think that's entirely uncommon, is it, my lady?"

"Not in the least uncommon, from what I can tell."

The maid bustled about with her cloth and soap and extra water, helping Belle get thoroughly clean while also keeping her hair dry. Belle didn't have time to wash, dry and style her hair if she wasn't to be unforgivably late that night, so she needed help. But it was clear to Belle that her personal servant was still thinking.

"Then what's the problem, m'lady? Surely you aren't bored already?" Ellen asked as she helped Belle from the tub and settled her in front of the mirror for her hair to be rearranged.

Despite her misgivings, Belle laughed. "Certainly not bored, no. But I will admit to missing home. It's not that, though. For some strange reason, my mother has decided she doesn't wish to escort unwed daughters any longer, so I must make haste and wed as soon as possible."

There was a moment of silence that accompanied Belle's words. The only sound in the room was the quiet swish of water as she washed.

"That does seem strange, my lady. I would have thought her ladyship would find it a lark to be taking you about. It's been a couple years since your sister got married. I'd think she would be happy to have another debutante in the house."

Isabelle shrugged and shook her head. "I don't really know. I thought the same thing. But she, and my father, too, seem to be most eager."

"And that leaves you in an awkward position, then, doesn't it?"

Belle was gratified by her maid's quick understanding.

"Are you feeling like you wasted your time, then?"

Belle nodded. "And now I feel rushed. As though I need to make this momentous decision with little information to go by."

The maid laughed. "So you were making one of your lists, then?"

Belle smiled into the mirror at her maid and shrugged, careful not to move her head while the woman was putting the final touches on her hairstyle.

"Have you narrowed down your possibilities, then? Or are you still working on it?"

"Promise you won't tell the others," Belle insisted.

The maid feigned offence. "My lady, I would never."

"Promise me, Ellen, or I won't tell you. I don't want one of the footmen saying something if one of these gentlemen were to call, nor do I want the maids tittering significantly. At least not until something were to become formal."

"I understand what you're saying, my lady," Ellen replied stiffly.

"I pray you, do not take offence. I do trust you with my secrets, but everything has been turned on its head this week. I cannot tell where to turn, and I am nearly at my wit's end."

The maid softened immediately and patted her mistress' shoulder. "Never mind about my feelings, my lady. I know it has been a burdensome time for you. I never should have ridden in the carriage with the luggage."

"I don't think you were given a choice, were you? And our time at Lord Simmons' hunting lodge was surprisingly not the worst I spent in the past several days, I can assure you. None of this is your fault, and knowing I have you to unburden myself to helps immensely. I should never have demanded your promise of silence. Of course, I know you can keep a secret."

"But I give you my promise anyway, and my apology for trying to be better than I am."

Belle smiled again at the other woman's wording. "You are better than most, Ellen. Don't let my missishness lead you to think otherwise." She stared toward the window for a moment before continuing. "In answer to your question, I am still working on who to consider. For one thing, I cannot even decide if Lord Simmons ought to be on my list."

"He's handsome, wealthy, and of good repute," Ellen pointed out.

"He is, that's true. But he hasn't shown the least bit of interest in me since I made my debut. Not even at the house party. It makes me think he isn't actually serious about finding his match. Or he took an aversion to me for some reason I cannot fathom." She lifted a shoulder. "I cannot say I consider either of those possibilities to be acceptable."

"No, of course not," the maid replied immediately as she gently powdered her mistress' face lightly. "I'd say he's off the list. You'd never wish to wed with a daft man, and surely he must be so if he didn't fall at your feet immediately."

Belle laughed as her heart lightened.

"Why, thank you, kind maiden," she said with a flick of her fan, batting her eyelashes in mock coquetry.

"Who else, then?"

"The list is woefully short, to be honest. Mr. Foster Northcott, Mr. Florent Alcott, and Lord Merton all became betrothed at the party. Mr. Alcott's younger brother has been a lovely dance partner a time or two this Season, but he is very obvious about his disinterest in wedding anytime soon. This is the problem as I see it. The gentlemen who were serious about marrying have already picked their ladies at the beginning of the Season.

The rest are merely toying with the idea. If only I had known."

"My dear lady, don't despair," Ellen pleaded even as she riffled through her mistress' wardrobe in search of the right gown for the evening. "If you turn your attention upon any eligible gentleman, you are sure to gain his attention and affection immediately."

"Now you are just playing it much too brown, Ellen," Isabelle said with a chuckle. "You will turn my head entirely with such compliments." Isabelle sighed. "There's also the small, little problem that I haven't the least idea how to go about turning my attention to an eligible gentleman in the way you suggest. My parents seem to think I ought to do so, as well. That if I just select one, and, I don't know, bat my eyelashes at him or some such nonsense, then he will come to heel, and we'll be done with it." Her laugh was tinged with despair. "I suspect it is not nearly that simple, for one thing. For another, that seems decidedly vulgar to me and what I understood in all my years growing up that I was not to do." She laughed again and lifted her hand in question. "What has changed so drastically that one of the things I was taught a lady ought to never do is suddenly the one thing I am most expected to do?"

The maid's face was filled with confused sympathy. "I can see how that would be bothersome, when you put it like that, my lady. But are you perhaps oversimplifying the matter? Or even maybe making it more complicated than it needs to be? I mean, isn't it just a matter of paying him some interest rather than expecting him to chase after you?"

Isabelle sighed. "But that's just the thing. I don't want to do that. I think he ought to do a little bit of chasing or he'll never appreciate me. If I chase after him, he'll resent me forever. If he chases after me, at least he can't blame me for it in later years."

Ellen stared at her mistress. "You don't anticipate a happy future in either case, do you, my lady?"

Belle tried to lighten the moment with laughter, but it fell short of the mark. "I suppose not."

"Perhaps if you figure out why that is, then you can figure out the rest of it. My parents seem quite happy with each other most of the time. I can't imagine wedding with someone I didn't anticipate happiness with. Why bother?"

Now Belle's laugh was much more genuine. "Why bother, indeed. You make it sound so simple, Ellen. But sadly, my marriage is more complicated than just finding someone I like and wedding with him. It is sadly a transaction of sorts. And all my life I've been told how important it is. My parents are suddenly trying to change the rules, and they want me off their hands. I think I would be better off trying to get to the bottom of *that* than anything else. It is much too important for me to rush into at this juncture." She stood up from the dressing table and embraced her maid quickly once more. "You have been most helpful, Ellen; thank you ever so much."

The maid laughed, blushed, and waved her away. “I didn’t do anything but brush your hair, and well, you know it.”

“It was everything. You showed an interest and helped me relax enough to think the matter through. And now I’ve decided. I won’t be rushed. I am firm on that. The rest can sort itself out. Short of father losing my dowry, there’s no need to rush. And if he did lose my dowry, no one would likely have me anyway, so it’s a moot matter.”

“Oh, my lady, I doubt it’s that.”

“Well, it’s something other than their ultimate desire to see their last daughter well wed, and I am determined to find out why. Their duty ought to be my protection, not seeing the back of me. But since I’ve had to entertain myself often as the youngest child, I am somewhat prepared to fend for myself in this matter and shan’t despair any longer. I will start immediately.”

“You shan’t do anything risky or dangerous, will you?”

Isabelle shrugged and laughed lightly. “Not likely, but this is a battle I am determined to win.” She twirled to check on the flowy nature of her skirt and then glanced back at her maid. “You’d best ensure you’re well rested, Ellen, as I’ll be in need of your company, I’m sure. Don’t let the housekeeper enlist you into too many other duties. You must explain that I’ve reserved you for myself.”

The maid returned her grin and dipped into a curtsy. “Try to enjoy your evening despite it all, my lady.”

Chapter Ten

A headache threatened behind Robert's eyes as he scanned the crowded ballroom. This was not where he truly wanted to be this evening. After the last few days of travel and unexpected companions, and now Lucy and Bert at home, he would rather be in his library with a decanter at his elbow and a dog at his knee. Or at one of his clubs trying to learn more about the conspiracy he was investigating.

But now was not the time to relax. He had wasted enough time. Robert needed a woman. Rather, he needed a wife, which in some ways was the same thing and in others, not in the least. Not just any woman would do. He needed someone who could take his sister in hand and then raise the next Viscount Simmons. A tall order, he knew.

How was he to find such a paragon on short notice? Especially whilst he was also supposed to be investigating the possibility of treason. The errant thought, which wasn't really errant, nearly distracted him from the purpose of his presence in said ballroom, but he pushed away the important but not currently pertinent thought. He would worry about Hudson and his schemes at another moment.

As his gaze scanned the crowd for what felt like the dozenth time, his eyes snagged upon the graceful figure of Lady Isabelle descending the stairs at Lady Bathurst's side. She was even more beautiful this evening than every other time he'd seen her. Robert couldn't fathom how that could possibly be the case, especially since she must surely be as tired as he or even more so considering she was female and had been in the company of his chatterbox sister all day.

But there she was, looking glorious and radiant. And determined? Was that a trick of the low lighting? Robert had seriously questioned whether the young lady had any involvement in the scheme to have the carriage "break down" right in front of his hunting lodge. She had seemed so truly innocent of the plan to entrap him, and he hadn't noticed any firm resolve in her face while she was at his house or even at Everleigh previously.

As it happened, she had struck him as somewhat pleasantly empty-headed at times while they were at Everleigh. Now though, even from a distance, he could see an intelligent gleam sparking her attention as she too scanned the crowd.

Had something happened in the few hours since they had seen one another?

Robert had been determined to keep the girl at arms' length due to her conniving parents. Now, he was torn between curiosity over the apparent change and worry that she, too, was as much of a schemer as his mother and her own. If it was only himself he had to worry about, he could just turn his back and ignore her, but since Lucy had taken such an interest in Lady Isabelle, that wasn't going to be so easy for him.

Having had enough of scheming women in his life, Robert had absolutely no intention of involving himself with another. He turned his back on the enticing picture of Lady Isabelle in a floaty frock of barely pink fabric. He was sure his sister would be able to wax poetic about the lady's gown and hairstyle. All Robert knew was that it was lovely.

But she was surely not the only beautiful woman present. And there were certainly more appropriate women for his needs in the room at that moment. He pulled his gaze back to scanning as he had been doing. He wasn't much more successful this time. His indecision was stymying him. He had no time for dithering. Lucy was already becoming ensconced in his home. The matter had turned from vaguely important to urgent in the span of three days.

With a determined nod, Robert set himself to action even as he cursed himself for his previous inattention. Even though he had been making the social rounds for years, he had evidently not been paying the matter nearly enough attention. He wasn't certain which matron would have the most knowledge to help him. But he knew enough to understand which of the older women present were particular friends with his mother. Despite his newfound determination to wed, he refused to allow the credit to be laid at his mother's feet, and he didn't want her to know that her schemes had likely worked until there was no avoiding it.

Until he had the banns read, he would keep his mother as ignorant as possible.

That might be a challenge with Lucy in the house but he was certainly going to give it a try.

Finally, his eyes fell upon Lady Bancroft—the oldest busybody Robert knew who also happened to hide the biggest heart in her interfering body. She had always had a soft spot for him. Robert suspected the old busybody had carried a torch for his father. She would surely help him. She would consider it a lark, to be sure.

"Simmons," Lady Bancroft greeted him with a scratchy voice that was barely above a croak in the hubbub of the crowded ballroom. "You are as dapper as ever, my boy."

Robert grinned. There was nothing like an old family friend to make one feel like a schoolboy despite the fact that he had inherited ten years earlier.

"My lady," Robert greeted as he bent over her hand with a flourish.

"Tell me what's on your mind, Simmons, as it's as evident as the nose on your face that you have a reason for seeking me out. It has been more than an age since I've had a visit from you, so I know it isn't just a greeting you wish to offer me."

Simmons fought an uncharacteristic blush that wanted to creep into his cheeks over her reprimand. He had also realised that he couldn't very well speak to her about his concerns in this venue if he wanted to keep the matter to himself.

"Can an old friend not say hello without there being a reason?"

"They can, of course, but don't forget that I've known you since you were born."

Robert grinned. He wasn't certain if that was entirely true, but it was near enough to being so that he didn't bother to quibble about it.

"I wonder if I might call on you."

Now Lady Bancroft's eyebrows lifted to nearly disappear inside the turban she had wound around her head. Curiosity glinted in her intelligent gaze.

"Of course, my boy. You've never required an invitation." It was both a reprimand and an invitation all rolled into one, keeping the grin in place on Robert's face.

"I should have said, I wonder when I might call on you, when we may be able to enjoy a comfortable coze."

Now Lady Bancroft cackled with delight, and she nearly rubbed her hands together with glee as she fully understood Robert wanted her assistance or advice. She would be thrilled to offer both.

"Does tomorrow morning suit? Come at some ungodly early hour before the rest of the gentry stir after an event such as this. Lord knows, I never sleep late. Or even early, for that matter," she grumbled before squeezing his hand. "I will look forward to it. And I'll ensure there's plenty of coffee as you're likely to need it."

Robert laughed and bowed over her hand once more, relieved that he had a plan of action. He went through the motions of the rest of the ball, dancing with various young ladies, wondering which would be the one Lady Bancroft would suggest for him. None of them stood out to him in particular which was a true shame.

And then he was forced to dance with Lady Isabelle.

Well, forced was far more melodramatic than the occasion called for, of course. But the circumstances, while he couldn't claim they had been contrived, certainly made him feel obliged to ask her to join him in the next dance. She had been standing unattended, without a partner, and he had already returned his previous partner to her mother. He hadn't yet asked anyone. It would have been churlish not to ask her.

"Are you having a good evening?" he asked, ignoring the sizzle that had shivered between them again, just like it had when he'd helped her from the carriage that afternoon. Could it be the same odd scenario? Had he rubbed fabric in a strange way? Or perhaps she had. But her hair didn't seem to be standing on end or anything as his had as a child when they'd done such foolish things. Robert tried not to frown as he awaited her answer to her question.

"I am trying to," came her odd answer before she flushed and stammered out another reply. "That is to say, of course, I am having a delightful evening. I am just fatigued from our travel, of course."

"I was surprised to see you in attendance, for that very reason."

"It does seem odd, doesn't it?" she murmured to Robert's amusement.

"This was an invitation you just couldn't refuse, I take it, then?"

Her tinkle of laughter did strange things to his insides, as usual, and he fought against the urge to pull her scandalously closer.

"Something like that, my lord," was all she would reply, despite her laughter. "What of you? I would have thought you would be home getting settled with Bert and Lucy."

"They found me exceedingly tiresome after their days of travel, I'm afraid."

"And so you thought a ball was just what you needed to unwind from the journey?"

"Much like you, I suppose."

Again, she laughed, but this time, she shook her head. "Somehow, I doubt that very much, my lord."

Robert wasn't sure if she was referring to the jest of unwinding at a Society ball or if it was his comment that their reasons for being there were the same, but it struck him that they probably were the same. She hadn't snagged herself a betrothal at the house party, so she was here to step up her ambitions. He wondered what had changed for the Bathurst family. He hadn't sensed any sort of urgency from Lady Isabelle when they'd first met. But to come out to a ball the night one had returned home after a day of travel? While he didn't believe women were as delicate as they were sometimes portrayed as being, he didn't think most ladies would make the effort unless sufficiently motivated.

What was motivating Lady Isabelle?

His heart went out to her. She wasn't that much older than his sister. She ought to be protected and coddled. A quick glance around the room showed him that rather than watching with happy indulgence, Lady Bathurst had a calculating expression of satisfaction upon her face, as though her daughter was exactly where she had sent her.

Robert trusted his own judgement enough to know that Lady Isabelle had not engineered his invitation to dance. But he also fully understood that he was on a shortlist of the most eligible bachelors of the Season. Any of the ladies he had danced with that evening would likely be happy to receive his addresses. He didn't think that in an arrogant matter. It was just the way things were in their world, whether one liked it or not.

"Which of the available ladies do you think would be suitable to assist me with my sister?"

Despite his usual calm self-control, Robert was surprised that these words had escaped his mouth. Isabelle appeared surprised, as well, but delighted, nonetheless, if the smile stretching her face was any indication.

"As a wife for you or an advisor?" she asked. Without waiting for his answer, she continued. "Because many of the matrons or widows would be thrilled to take your sister in hand, but they might not make you the best partner."

Robert grinned. As he had begun to suspect, she wasn't the empty-headed simpleton he had thought upon first introduction.

"I'm not really thinking to hire her a companion. Although, if truth be told, that might be a better idea than the one I had."

"Did you think to wed someone who could take her on?" she asked him with wise perception shining from her watchful gaze. "That would solve your short-term problem but not necessarily be a good thing for the longer term."

Robert tried not to frown. She was merely voicing what he had been worrying about himself. But surely he wasn't so far off the mark with his thoughts for his future.

"I may not be the best one to offer you advice on this matter," Isabelle added in a gentle tone. "But I am almost certain you could find someone who might work well in both cases; you just might have to look in the less obvious locations."

"Do you mean other than a ballroom?"

"No, perhaps other than the dance floor of the ballroom."

When he quirked an eyebrow at her, she laughed again. "You might be looking for a wallflower or a young widow. Someone perhaps a bit more experienced. Socially acceptable, thus here at a Society function, but not necessarily spending the entire evening dancing."

While it had been exactly his own thought, somehow, the lady's ready agreement or acceptance of his fate irked him. Robert didn't want to wed a wallflower. Nor did he see himself marrying a widow. Not that he thought widows were unworthy, he just pictured himself with a younger, less experienced woman, perhaps one who would look up to him. He wondered if that made him dismally antiquated. He almost shook his head but didn't want to confuse the woman currently in his arms.

"So you don't think a debutante would be able to handle Lucy?"

Robert couldn't identify what was going through his own mind. He was acting foolishly all of a sudden. To his surprise, though, Isabelle didn't recoil or frown over his question but looked pensive for a moment even while the dance separated them. He was delighted to note that she barely conversed with her next partner, merely smiling at him charmingly while appearing quite preoccupied.

"I most certainly think some debutantes would be delighted to have your sister as her new family. If you are careful and choose wisely, you will find the exact right one." She paused again before adding, "I, of course, am of the opinion that most women can handle just about anything if they have to. Some will do so with more joy than others."

And that hit the subject right on the nose, striking Robert mute for a moment. What was he to say to that? He wanted a house filled with joy. He had never realised it but that was exactly his determination. He wasn't certain if he had ever experienced a joy-filled home, but it was his new goal in life. And he had Lady Isabelle to thank for it.

"How does one find such a creature?" He hadn't meant to ask the question aloud, but again, the girl's light laughter delighted him.

"There's the rub, isn't it? I have the same question about the gentlemen."

"At least you don't have the same encumbrances as I find myself with."

"You think not?" she asked as her gaze flickered toward her mother. She quickly hid her thoughts with a practised smile. "I suppose not. As the youngest sibling in my family, and with both my parents still alive, my circumstances are far different from yours, it is true."

"And yet, we both find ourselves in search of a mate."

"Such an odd condition, is it not?"

Robert chuckled. He supposed she was right. He could have talked with her all evening, but he could hear their dance coming to an end. He tried not to be disappointed. She was not for him. He needed to look for his joyful bride elsewhere.

With a bow, he took his leave of her as the last notes were played.

Chapter Eleven

Belle fought to keep her eyes from following Lord Simmons from the room. The ball was nearing its end, and he appeared to be taking his leave. She ought to collect her mother and do the same. It would not do to be a straggler. And she was exhausted on every level. It was a marvel she had managed to stay so late as it was.

"You did well," Lady Bathurst complimented on the drive to their townhouse, much to Belle's surprise. "I thought you were reluctant to attend this evening, but you managed to be partnered for every dance."

"That wasn't such a change from previous balls," Belle remarked.

"No, but previously it seemed as though your heart wasn't in it. I think you'll see a difference in your reception after this."

Belle gritted her teeth. If her parents had been forthcoming about their determination to marry her off as soon as possible, perhaps she could have found a suitable mate as soon as they had arrived.

She fought a sense of defeat and disappointment as she wondered if she'd missed out on a better choice.

She refused to give in to despair. She only needed one. She didn't care to be the girl who could say she had turned down dozens of proposals. That would only appear mean-spirited in her opinion. But obviously she did need that one.

"What will happen if I don't find a match? Will I need to seek employment?" she hadn't expressed her view on her parents' rush to them, but she found, in her tired state, her tongue was looser than usual.

"Don't be daft, Isabelle. You will not seek employment. And you will not remain unwed. You just need to put a little effort into it. This is serious business, not a lark."

"I understand that it's not a lark. What I don't understand is why I must rush into the decision and why it is suddenly an urgent matter. I was never given the least inkling that there was a need for me to wed quickly. I had thought to perhaps wait until next year, so I haven't been giving the matter my full, serious attention. It leaves me feeling decidedly wrong-footed."

"Well, that was your mistake, wasn't it? I don't see how anyone could think coming up for the Season is anything other than urgent business."

Belle held her tongue for a moment before mentioning, "It is my understanding that many women come to Town for the Season who are already wed. I have met some of them, in fact. They often host balls and routs and such. So I don't think every single person present in Town is here in search of a husband or wife."

"It doesn't matter what everyone else is doing, Isabelle. It is what you do that counts. You must find yourself a good match. As soon as possible, if you will."

Belle bit her lip, wondering once more how to deal with the strange situation.

"Are you in some sort of trouble? Do we need financial help? Could we not sell something or go to a bank?"

"You have returned to being tiresomely daft, Isabelle, and I cannot bear it. Do hush for now."

Belle's mouth shut with a snap. She wasn't being daft. It was a valid question. She was a person. While being a female person meant she didn't have all the same rights as a man, she was nearly certain she could not literally be forced into marriage against her will. She wasn't certain how she could verify that understanding, but she would do so, even as she sought out her future husband.

It wasn't that she was opposed to wedding. She wasn't daft as her mother kept accusing her of being. It was obvious that was the way of life—one grew up and left home to marry. But she had never thought that it was to be something she must rush into without careful consideration as though it were just a task to be gotten over with. It was her entire future life at stake. Surely her parents couldn't honestly be wishing her to just accept anyone.

Belle sighed. It didn't really matter what her parents thought. If she didn't wed before the Season ended, or at least find herself a betrothed, even if her parents allowed her to return to Bathurst, she would no longer be comfortable there knowing they wished her elsewhere.

She feared she would never be comfortable again.

It would be strange to make her home somewhere new with a gentleman she didn't yet know. New servants, new surroundings, a new family. Why had she never given it thought before? Perhaps she was just as daft as her mother said.

The view outside her window blurred as tears filled her eyes, but she quickly dashed them away. She wasn't going to turn into a watering pot no matter the provocation.

How hard could it be? Many of her acquaintances had found their match quickly. While Belle had turned her attention elsewhere, she hadn't really paid attention to how they had done it, but surely, as her mother had said, now that she had turned her focus to the matter, she could manage it, as well.

Her list wasn't very long, though. In fact, it was appallingly short. She did think it vulgar to set her cap at a gentleman. But perhaps she could figure out a way to set herself in one of their paths. She would have her maid do some investigating. It might be difficult, but surely it was far from impossible.

Belle's spirits brightened. It was always best to have a plan. Hers might be flimsy at best, but it was a plan, and with a bit of effort and ingenuity, she would have this matter sorted long before Town emptied for the summer.

"Thank you for waiting up, Ellen; you are surely as tired or more than I am."

"I would be nowhere else, my lady. And with your not returning when I expected, I have had lighter duties than usual the past couple of days."

Belle smiled. "At least there was a benefit to someone for that mishap."

"Did you have a nice evening, my lady? Since you are late returning, I would expect so."

"It was fine," Belle answered. "We were late arriving, of course, since we were travelling today. So we didn't linger there as long as it would seem. Some just thought we had been at some other entertainment earlier—that was how late we arrived. But I danced nearly every number while we were there, so you could say it was a successful evening."

"But did you enjoy it, my lady?" the maid asked, sounding puzzled.

Belle lifted her shoulder in a shrug and sighed. "I cannot say, to be honest, Ellen." She stood quietly while the maid helped her out of her gown and took down her hair. Once she was seated at her dressing table, she watched in the mirror as the servant brushed out her hair. "I am uncertain if anything will be enjoyable with this burden hanging over my head. This sense of urgency makes me anxious, to tell the truth. I have never felt quite like this before."

The maid nodded in sympathy. "It does sound quite dreadful. But you have your plan, don't you?"

"Such as it is," Belle replied. "I'm going to need your help. I need you to look into Lord Hudson."

"What do you mean by look into him? I don't think I have it in me to turn secret agent."

"No, no, but if you could perhaps find out from his servants what his routine is like, I could find myself in his company a little more often and get to know him, you see."

Ellen brightened. "That is quite a brilliant idea, my lady."

"It would probably be best if you take one of the footmen with you so you aren't out alone. I would hate to see something happen to you."

"Is it likely to be dangerous, then?" Ellen frowned. "Why did you settle on him?"

"I didn't settle on him specifically. But my list is short. He is the first I thought to look into. And no, I don't think you will be particularly in danger, but any young woman wandering about Town by herself is in a certain amount of danger, wouldn't you say?"

The maid shrugged. "You would be far more so than me, my lady, but I appreciate your concern. And perhaps he could do some asking, too."

"There you go. You could be an investigative duo." Belle laughed, her first sensation of genuine mirth since she had left the company of Miss Lucretia. Oddly, she missed the chattering girl. But not her older, glowering brother. She was beyond embarrassed over her parents' actions and couldn't bear his disapproving stare. He had been pleasant enough at the ball that night, but despite his eligibility, Belle didn't have Lord Simmons on her list of potential suitors, no matter what her parents thought. If nothing else, she was determined that her husband not disapprove of her for the rest of her days. If she was forced into marriage with anyone, that was likely to be the circumstance she would find herself in. She needed a gentleman to think he was fortunate to have her. It was highly unlikely Lord Simmons would ever experience that sensation.

But he had been a delightful dance partner, Belle mused as she climbed up into her bed. He was the perfect height so that she felt delicate in his arms. He was clearly strong and fit well in his coat. His hair appeared thick and all his. Its luster had made her think of touching it for the briefest moment. That would have caused an uncomfortable stir, she thought with amusement as she drifted off to sleep even as the sound of the music they had danced to ran through her memories and accompanied her into her dreams.

Chapter Twelve

"Well, at least you can follow directions," Lady Bancroft called out as Robert was shown into her salon. "I like that in a man."

Robert grinned as he bent over the bony hand she held out imperiously. "I was taught it wouldn't do to keep a lady waiting."

Lady Bancroft harumphed but appeared pleased despite her effort to sound grudging.

"You are looking tired, Simmons; you need a wife." The lady certainly didn't beat around the bushes or try to sugarcoat her words.

Robert laughed. "I don't see how the two subjects relate, but it is fortuitous that you would say so as that is exactly why I have sought out your advice at this ungodly hour when you are sure to not have visitors."

"Very wise, my boy. You surely need advice and cannot rely on that flighty piece who is your mother to offer any wisdom for you."

Robert knew he ought to defend his mother from such words, but he couldn't very well argue with them since that was exactly why he was in Lady Bancroft's salon that morning. He merely held his silence and waited for her to continue.

"Why now? What has changed now, in the middle of the Season, when previous years and even at the beginning of this one, you couldn't be bothered to seriously consider taking a wife?"

It was a good question. This was why he had sought out Lady Bancroft. He knew she would get to the heart of it with him. And keep his confidences if he were to offer any.

"Lucy and Bert have decided they no longer wish to live with our mother and her new husband."

"Ah, I see. And of course, Lucretia needs a woman in the house. You could send her to school," Lady Bancroft offered.

"I could. But I still need to pick a school, and she'll need clothes and every manner of things I cannot even begin to think of."

"You could seek advice on that, my boy; no need to get leg-shackled if you aren't ready yet. Don't do it for your sister. She'll be grown in a couple of years, but your wife will be forever."

Robert ran a hand through his hair and paced away from the settee. "I know, this is the problem. I do need a wife. Seeing my brother, who is currently my heir, so young and carefree on one hand but worried about Lucy on the other, I don't want to add to his shoulders the need to train to take over the estate. He needs to be one or the other—second son or heir. I don't want to leave him in this limbo at his age. And I do have Lucy to think of. And I will need an heir anyhow so why not now?"

"But that's why you've come to me. You have a very unique situation to navigate. I understand now. You want a wife who will last, but also one who can help you with your current situation. This is challenging but surely not impossible." She paused in thought. "Could I be so bold as to ask why you have resisted searching out a wife before now? You reached your majority some time ago, to be sure."

Robert smiled over her question about boldness. He had never known of Lady Bancroft not to be bold. But it was sweet of her to ask his permission. He liked her immensely even though he knew many in the *ton* feared her.

"My mother. I didn't want to do her bidding," he finally admitted, much to her delight if the crowing laughter was any indication, but she sobered when he added, "And I don't want to follow my father's footsteps."

"I can understand that," she answered when she finally had her mirth under control. "Very well, I didn't know about the children when I was thinking about it, but it doesn't change my thoughts overmuch. The ladies I have in mind for you should be able to take it in stride."

Robert shouldn't have been surprised. Of course the wise old woman would have an inkling as to why he was seeking her council. He was even more pleased with himself for seeking her out.

"There's Inglewood's daughter, Lady Chloe. She is a bit too serious for your young sister, perhaps, but she would be a steadying influence to be sure. And would make a perfect viscountess for you. She seems more interested in wedding this year now that it is her second Season. She's not so young as some of the others but not old or jaded by any means."

For the life of him, Robert couldn't even draw a mental image of the woman. Had they even met? Surely they must have if she was making the rounds, but she had obviously not made much of an impression.

"There's also Lady Isabelle, Bathurst's daughter." Lady Bancroft didn't notice Robert's reaction or at least she didn't remark upon it as she continued. "Her parents seem a touch irregular this Season, but that shouldn't matter to you."

"Why shouldn't that matter? I already have one parent in my life who is a touch irregular."

Lady Bancroft laughed. "That you do, my boy, that you do. So you ought to know how to handle them. And everyone's parents are a touch irregular when looked at from different angles. I doubt if you shall find a wife without, unless she were an orphan, and then where would you be?"

Robert grinned. "Do you know any orphans?"

"Don't be cheeky, young man; this is serious."

"Don't I know it?" Robert agreed wholeheartedly. "Do you have any other suggestions for me?"

"I don't think you ought to wed to help your sister. You ought to wed to please yourself."

"So you don't think accomplishing both at once is possible?"

"It might be with either of the two young ladies I suggested, but it is a huge proposition you are requesting, and I'm not certain any young woman who would make you the most suitable wife is also going to be the best companion for your sister. And that should be perfectly acceptable. Lucretia has been dealt a bad hand as have you and your brother. But such is life. You shouldn't be condemned for it."

Robert shrugged. "I need to look after them."

"That is commendable, Simmons, but you can surely do that without a wife. Or with a wife of your own choosing. She doesn't have to be the solution to Lucy's problem. Lucy would probably benefit greatly from a year or two at a finishing school, anyway. Who knows what your mother has filled her head with?"

"But I don't want to send her away as soon as she has arrived. She will think I don't want her, no matter how I explain it."

"Then do your best to make her feel welcome and then send her away when you think she's settled into the new circumstances."

Robert could tell the older woman was becoming impatient with him, but he was unwilling to concede to her suggestions. He tried to smooth the situation over.

"I most certainly appreciate your suggestions and support, my lady. I will give serious thought to what you have said." He waved a hand elegantly. "Now tell me how you have been. And please accept my sincere apologies that I didn't lead with that."

"No need to bamboozle me, young man. I'm not likely to be your next viscountess."

Robert laughed as he knew she expected and tried not to shudder at the thought. She was a dear woman but also the most managing one he had ever met. He wondered what she had been like as a girl. He suspected she had been friends with his grandparents. She had always been friendly with his father and then with him when he'd entered Society, making him feel welcome when he was a grieving, bewildered new viscount trying to fill his father's shoes both on the estate and in the House of Lords.

The passing of time could change so much. He now felt very at home in the roles he had taken on. Except this new role. He had been his siblings' guardian in name only for nearly all of the past ten years. Now, taking a hands-on position with them was going to be a whole other story. His brother really needed to be in school. But he could understand and appreciate Bert's reluctance to leave Lucy. That was commendable. But he needed to make Lucy feel comfortable enough that Cuthbert would be willing to go away. It was going to be a challenge for certain. How he was to find the time amongst all his other responsibilities was his concern.

After having the promised cup of coffee and listening to Lady Bancroft's gossip, Robert took his leave.

Lady Isabelle? How could the wise older woman make such a misguided suggestion?

Robert shook his head as he climbed up into his curricle. He had other things he needed to see to that day. He was glad Lady Bancroft had suggested he see her so early. While it had been a challenge to rise with the birds, he had already seen to this appointment, and still, there was plenty of day left to him.

He was on his way back to his townhouse after visiting his solicitor and stopping in at Whites when he saw an odd sight. If he wasn't mistaken, the footman he was looking at was wearing the Bathurst livery, and the young woman at his side was Lady Isabelle's personal maid. Robert's gaze narrowed. The pair appeared to be following Lord Hudson. *How very irregular,* he thought. They were far from experts in subterfuge, so it was unlikely Hudson hadn't noticed, but he carried on about his business as though he was oblivious of their presence.

Were they following the man at Lady Isabelle's behest? For what possible purpose? Did they know he was suspected of being a foreign agent? *Was Lady Isabelle an agent?*

That was highly unlikely. The Home Office was determined to always put the nation's interests first, but they had a couple of scruples left about how they went about their activities, and one of them included always protecting ladies. So it was highly doubtful they would employ one of them.

But stranger things had been witnessed, Robert reflected, during his time with the Office. There was also the possibility that the lady had also been approached by foreign agents. They had far less scruples than the English, Robert knew. They would, in fact, delight over the thought of having turned a gently reared woman against her own.

Of course, Robert mused, he might be seeing shadows where none existed. While that pair was most definitely Lady Isabelle's servants, they could be on a completely innocuous errand that had nothing to do with Lord Hudson or anything to do with national affairs. Or they could be looking to join a life of crime, apart from Lady Isabelle, and were thinking to lighten the nobleman's pockets.

If the traffic weren't so dense and if he wouldn't be far too obvious, Robert would get down and follow the trio, but that would draw too much attention.

Robert sighed. It was one more thing he would have to take care of. And now he would need to spend more time with Lady Isabelle in order to get to the bottom of the matter. There was no other way around it. He ignored the sense of anticipation that filled him along with the whisper at the back of his mind that was telling him he could set his own servants onto the matter. No, he told himself firmly, this was an issue he had to see to himself. As a member of the nobility, surely he owed her that respect at least.

Chapter Thirteen

Belle was pacing impatiently around her bedchamber in her father's London townhouse when her maid finally returned. She had used to consider it her home away from home even though she hadn't in reality stayed there that often. That sense of homecoming was long gone now, though.

"You haven't gone and worked yourself into a fret, have you, my lady? We tried not to take too long."

Belle waved away Ellen's concerns. "Don't trouble yourself over me, I beg of you. I cannot help fretting under the circumstances, but you weren't longer than you should have been, don't worry."

"You ought to not worry, either. This is a terrible situation for you to be in, and I worry for you, my lady."

Belle hugged her maid quickly. The young servant had been with her for years, having started as a kitchen assistant but was quickly promoted upstairs when the girls had grown close.

"Never mind about my troubled mind; it's likely to be a constant state until I sort my situation to both my mother's and my own liking. The sad truth is that Lord Hudson isn't even the only gentleman I want you to check on for me, so I will need to be well fortified. Did you manage to find anything out?"

"I'll want you to tell me why you chose him, for one thing, my lady. For another, I'm not really sure how helpful it will be to you, but yes, we found out that Lord Hudson spends an extraordinary amount of time at his club. But that is not somewhere you can go. We did find out that he usually walks through the same park every day so that might help. We could go and linger there in the hopes that we will run into him. But we also found out that he has accepted an invitation to the musicale being hosted by Lady Bancroft in two nights. I believe you also received an invitation."

"I think we might have declined that invitation, though," Belle said with a frown.

"Is it possible to write to her ladyship and rescind your declination?"

Belle laughed at the odd wording but she shook her head. "I'm not sure if that would be acceptable. I will check with Mother if we did in fact decline before I decide how *gauche* it might be to request a change of plans. It is possible I'm mistaken about the invitation. I wasn't paying so much attention to the Season before our trip to Everleigh."

"I know." The maid nodded in sympathy as she began getting her mistress ready for callers. "Shall we venture out later to see what you think of that park?"

Belle nodded gently, not to dislodge the maid's hands in her hair. "You did well, Ellen; thank you for finding that out for me. Was it difficult?"

"Not really. We just followed him and asked a few questions on each end. He pretty much went straight from his house to his club, so it wasn't difficult."

Isabelle smiled. She would bring the two servants with her when she left the household, she determined. They would be her only familiar faces. Aside from whomever she wed, of course. But at present, she didn't even know who that would be so her thought stood sound. Her future husband was not yet a familiar face.

"As to your question of why I chose Hudson, it's mostly because he has given me the impression of being calm and kind when we've encountered one another. He is not exceptionally fashionable and doesn't seem to make long-winded speeches about nonsense. He is also rumoured to be seeking a wife, so I shan't have to convince him. Despite my mother's insistence, I have no intention of pursuing a gentleman in reality."

"I should think not," Ellen promptly responded, sounding scandalised at the very thought. "Oh, you received messages, my lady." Ellen suited her words to action, pulling a piece of paper from her pocket.

"How delightful," Belle pronounced as she scanned the page. "It's from Lucy. She wants to visit." Belle laughed as she read the jumbled words on the girl's short note. "How I wish you had been with us at Lord Simmons' lodge. You would have enjoyed his sister as much as I did."

The servant didn't comment. It was unlikely she would have a chance to meet the girl. Her life was so much different from that of her childhood companion.

"I don't see why she couldn't visit after we've made our calls," Belle continued. "Perhaps we could stop at her house and collect her. I am afraid she will set out on her own without even a maid to lend her countenance."

"Is she a child or a young lady?" Ellen asked, causing Belle to lightly laugh anew.

"Both, I would say. I didn't ask her for her years directly, but I would guess she is thirteen or fourteen. Perhaps even fifteen. Too young to make her debut, of course, but not exactly a nursery child. It is an awkward age at the best of times, I think."

"As I recall, you did just fine through that period in your own life," the loyal maid insisted.

"Perhaps, but I was also the third girl in the family rather than the first. And my family has only become strange in recent days, not when I was a girl. Miss Lucretia lost her father when she was still in the nursery, and now her mother has remarried. That must be difficult for her to deal with, I would expect. I would find it difficult to deal with at my age, let alone when I was much younger. And I have a reasonably close relationship with my brothers and sisters. Miss

Lucy's brother, who is now her guardian, is at least a decade older than her, from what I can tell—probably more like fifteen years older. That would make for a more distant relationship, wouldn't you think?"

"Poor girl," Ellen softened. "What shall you do for her?"

Isabelle sighed. "There isn't a great deal I can do for her, to be honest. She cannot make her debut yet so I cannot have her accompany me on visits or anything like that. But we can perhaps go shopping or to the circulating library or other such things. There is the difficulty that I don't much care for her brother."

Ellen laughed. "Why is that? Is he not an eligible gentleman? He should have been on your list."

Belle sighed again. "He is, truth be told, although I didn't actually put his name in writing," she admitted. "But not for my truly wishing him there. He is just so perfectly acceptable. It is too bad that he thinks I am a deceptive trickster."

"Ah, the broken carriage wheel." Ellen nodded and then shrugged. "Surely he could be convinced of your innocence."

"I'm not sure about that. How do I go about convincing him I am innocent of something I'm not completely sure even happened? Besides, he doesn't strike me as the forgiving type despite his welcome of his young brother and sister. And even his welcome of us into his home so unexpectedly. He didn't really have a choice in either case. He was reasonably gracious, I suppose, but he doesn't really strike me as one I'd be comfortable meeting in the breakfast room every day for the rest of my life."

Ellen smiled at her mistress in the mirror. "I'm certain you realise it's even more complicated than that."

Heat filled Belle's cheeks but she merely nodded. "To be sure. But it is the everyday life that you have to really share with someone you make your family with. I need a man to want to have me there, not take me on sufferance."

"We will do our best to find the right gentleman; have no fear."

The prickle of tears tingled behind Belle's eyes. Her servant was being kinder to her than her own family had been. It was disconcerting to say the least. She ought to have been comfortable having this conversation with her mother. In fact, her mother ought to be initiating this conversation with *her* rather than berating her for not having formed an alliance yet.

Belle had no thought to selecting a gentleman on her own. She truly had not thought the matter through sufficiently before they'd come up to Town, it would seem. She had been under the murky impression that several gentlemen would present themselves to her, and she would be left with the perhaps uncomfortable privilege of picking between them.

Instead, she hadn't been a huge success. No gentlemen had yet offered for her. She hadn't been troubled by that as she hadn't thought the matter dramatically urgent. But her parents were leading her to change her understanding of the matter without offering her any guidance or assistance.

That was fine, Belle insisted to herself. It was better if she figured it out on her own anyhow. She was the one who would have to live with whatever came of it, after all.

“Thank you, Ellen, you have done marvels as always, with my appearance. Will you accompany Mother and me on our calls?”

“No, my lady, unless you expressly request it. The housekeeper has some tasks she expects me to assist with.”

“I trust you aren’t being overworked?” Belle asked, worried.

“No, my lady, not in the least. While I wouldn’t mind accompanying you as it would get me out of helping sort the linen chests, sitting in the foyer while you visit isn’t the most exciting prospect, either.”

“Oh dear, I can see your point. Very well, but don’t allow Mrs. Frampton to overwork you.”

“Never fear that, my lady. But I shall accompany you to the park to waylay Lord Hudson. Thomas will come, too. When he found out what we were doing, he didn’t feel it right that you and I go without an escort.”

“What could possibly happen to us?” Belle scoffed at the thought.

“I shan’t fill your head with the suggestions Thomas made as to what could happen, but I decided that I don’t fully disagree with him.”

Belle stared at her servant in indecision. She thought it might look ridiculous for her to go about with two servants in tow. But what if they were correct?

"We are country bred, my lady, and perhaps not as up to snuff as we'd like to think. If he says we ought to be accompanied, perhaps we ought to listen."

"Are you turning sweet on the footman, Ellen?" Belle asked, torn between delight and worry for her friend.

"Whether I am or not is not at all the point of this conversation. I certainly wouldn't involve you in that if I were; now don't be a ninny."

Belle burst into laughter at the familiarity of the servant. "I will try hard to curb my ninnyish inclinations, my dear girl. And this first time I will accept Thomas's escort as I don't have the lay of the land as it were. We can decide between us how we feel about venturing forth another time." She paused in thought for a moment. "And I will tell Thomas that I appreciate his concern for our safety," she added with a grin. Whether it was concern for his mistress or her servant, Belle still appreciated anyone caring enough to offer caution. It seemed to be in short supply in the household of late.

Without much further dithering, Belle took her leave of the servant, joining her mother for their round of morning calls. Before they left, Isabelle was thrilled to see that a number of bouquets and posies had been delivered for her. She hadn't received so many gifts or tributes since her very first foray into Society at the beginning of the Season.

"I told you how well you did last night," Lady Bathurst commented smugly as she surveyed the collection on the front table.

Belle quickly read each note to see who had sent what. If they were to encounter any of the gentlemen on their rounds, she wanted to be able to acknowledge his gift. She ignored her whisper of disappointment that none of them were from Lord Simmons. It was ridiculous of her to even give the man a single thought. It was just her concern for his sister that had him on her mind, she assured herself as she followed her mother from the house.

It was good that she had taken the time to note the gifts as one of the drawing rooms they were shown into was nearly overflowing with gentlemen callers. Belle wasn't sure if she was disappointed or delighted. Obviously Lady Chloe was the most popular young lady from the night before. She should have paid more attention to which calls her mother wanted to make. Belle wished they hadn't called on such a popular debutante that day. She didn't want it to appear as though she were looking to steal the attention rightfully directed at the other lady.

But despite her wish to claim otherwise, it would seem for debutantes, the Season really was a competition. A popularity contest as it were. Belle hated that concept. To her mind, this wasn't a game they were playing. It was their futures, and the lives of their future children, at stake. Did it really matter that Lady Chloe received twenty-five deliveries that morning and Lady Isabelle only ten or fifteen? To some, it would obviously matter a great deal. To Belle's mind, they each only needed one suitor as long as he was the right one.

There ought to be an application process, she thought with suppressed amusement as she went through the room distributing greetings, trying not to sigh over the ridiculousness of the ritual. None of the occupants of the room truly cared about her as a person as far as she could tell although she knew some of the gentlemen at least appeared pleased to see her if somewhat embarrassed to be discovered courting both of the popular ladies.

Belle did her best not to allow it to disturb her equilibrium. She still didn't know any of the gentlemen well. She certainly couldn't make a claim on any of them. If they wished to send posies to both ladies or even all the ladies they'd danced with the night before, it was their pocketbook that would suffer for it, not her.

She kept that thought firmly in mind as she sat in the spot Lady Chloe was coyly patting next to her even as her stomach sank. Belle was not looking forward to the next ten or fifteen minutes of her life.

"The colour of your gown is one of my very favourites," Chloe almost cooed over her, making Belle feel even more uncomfortable, which was unfortunate. She was sure the other young lady had intended to set her at ease, or at the very least, Belle was almost certain the compliment was intended to be sincere. Instead, though, it made Belle feel awkward. Was it sincere? Did the other girl wish she owned Belle's dress? Was she going to ask for the direction of her seamstress? Should she admit she had brought the gown from home?

Belle clamped down on her frantic thoughts and offered the most pleasant smile she could muster.

"That is kind of you to say. I am quite partial to any shade of pink, as well. But I can see from your colouring, it would particularly suit you."

To Belle's surprise, Chloe's smile widened even as she shook her head. "I think pink is the best colour because it suits just about everyone, don't you think? It's a shame we're expected to wear varying shades of white or lights. I think it should be pink for all debutantes. It would be to everyone's advantage."

Belle couldn't help laughing. "Except perhaps redheads."

Chloe's eyes widened further, and a small snort escaped her. She quickly placed a hand over her mouth as her shoulders shook with mirth. "Fortunately, they are quite rare."

Belle returned the other girl's smile and nodded. "True. I don't think there are any this year making their debut, so your suggestion could work well. Who should we speak to?"

"One of the patronesses, to be sure."

Belle tilted her head and tapped her chin in mock thought. "Perhaps Lady Jersey?"

"No, no, the Princess, just to be safe."

They dissolved into giggles, immediately fast friends.

Belle's heart lifted. Even though the Season felt competitive and she was out of sorts with her parents' intentions for her future, feeling as though she had made a friend set her a little more at ease in her situation.

"Do you know everyone who is here?" Chloe enquired, preparing to make introductions.

Belle glanced around. She had been introduced to everyone at her first few large events and now felt as though she were acquainted with everyone even though in some ways it felt as though she knew no one. She nodded, and the other young woman grimaced.

"Of course, you do, forgive me."

Belle frowned. "There is nothing to forgive. You wanted me to be comfortable; that is to be thanked, not forgiven."

"You aren't the usual sort, are you?" Lady Chloe remarked before their quiet *tete a tete* was interrupted by one of the gentlemen.

"You two ought to be paying us your attention, not each other," Lord Brutus complained. Belle was fairly certain he had meant to sound teasing, but instead, it struck her as mean-spirited. She was relieved he hadn't made it onto her shortlist of eligible potential husbands. She couldn't bear the thought of a mean-tempered husband.

"Ladies always need one another, my lord; surely you must realise that," Lady Chloe rebuked him very gently. "But do forgive my inattention; I didn't mean to be inhospitable. I believe you were telling everyone about some sporting event?"

With that, the young woman gently steered the conversation in a positive direction, and Belle could only admire her ability. She knew if it had been her, she would have felt wrong-footed by the gentleman's words and would have been in a hurry to smooth the matter over. She could see that Lady Chloe was far more experienced than she was, and she nearly sighed in dismay.

Her parents were in a hurry to marry her off, but Belle suspected she wasn't suited for the position of anyone's wife quite yet, especially not a nobleman who might need a hostess. She mentally scanned her list to see whom she had selected. Were there any appropriate gentlemen who might not have inherited and who didn't take their seat in the House? Perhaps they wouldn't need as skilled a hostess, she mused even as she joined into the flow of the conversation. As far as she knew, the thought niggled at the back of her mind: Lord Hudson didn't have a seat in the house despite his title. It was merely a courtesy title he was granted as his father's heir, who was still very much alive.

With that, the time flew quickly, and before she knew it, Lady Bathurst had gained her feet and was beckoning for Belle to join her.

Belle made no objections. She wished she hadn't promised Lucy she would collect her for a visit. Belle was eager to get on with her effort to become acquainted with Lord Hudson. While a part of her knew one more day shouldn't make a great difference when viewed from the perspective of the rest of her life, another part worried that he would settle his attentions on some other young woman in the meantime.

She had to push those worries from her mind. The same could be said of any gentleman. Such thoughts could not be borne. Such a way madness lay.

"What a delightful woman Lady Inglewood is," Lady Bathurst was enthusing as they settled into the carriage. "I nearly overstayed; I was having such a pleasant visit." Belle noticed that her mother didn't bother asking if she was having a pleasant visit. That thought arrested her attention. Perhaps her parents truly were just over being parents. They didn't want to have to put others' interests ahead of their own any longer as had been their wont for all of Belle's life. Now her mother wanted to make her own friendships, not contingent on whether or not the other lady had children of an appropriate age to play with the Bathurst children.

While Belle wished wholeheartedly they had been able to bear up for one more year, she supposed she couldn't blame them for being tired of putting themselves last. With their six children, and Belle the youngest, it had been a long time since they had been carefree youths.

Did all older people wish to return to their youth? Belle wondered absently as she gazed out the window as the carriage made its slow way through the traffic.

Collecting Miss Lucretia took barely a moment as the dear girl had been eagerly awaiting them and was ready to go as soon as the knocker sounded. Belle was gratified at her eagerness and all the more determined to help the young girl despite her own worries. Surely she could manage to do both now that she had enlisted the help of her maid and footman with the other project.

Chapter Fourteen

"What do you mean my sister is out? Out where? With whom? Did you make sure she was accompanied?" Robert tried not to bellow his questions at the servants who surely couldn't be expected to restrain the girl if she had a mind to do something he had forbidden.

"I don't like to speak ill of the lady, but she led us to believe you had granted your permission for her to go visiting with Lady Bathurst and her daughter, my lord."

"Ah, I see. Did Lady Bathurst come for Lucretia?" He could see Lucy leading the servants to believe that, and really, he hadn't truly denied her. It wasn't the servant's fault his sister had finagled the situation.

"She remained in the carriage. It was Lady Isabelle who knocked on the door."

"Very well, thank you. I will collect Lucy myself then."

"They did mention that they would return her after their visit."

"I can save them the trip, in that case," Robert replied with firm conviction. He shuddered at the thought of his sister spending an extended time with more conniving women than she had grown up with.

He shouldn't think so ill of their mother, but all his life, he could remember her schemes and stratagems. It had been a drain on his and his father's relationship when he was a boy as she had often tried to come between them after she had moved back in with them after such an extended absence. It was odd for a mother to be jealous of her children, but that was the only explanation Robert could make for his mother's behaviour. With the passage of time, and with eyes of maturity, Robert could see that his mother must have been, and likely still was, a very insecure woman. She wanted her husband's undivided attention and acted out when she didn't receive it. It was an unrealistic expectation for a viscount's wife and had led to all manner of problems. But in either case, Lucy had obviously learned some of her behaviours if her departure from the house that day was any indication.

And Lady Bathurst seemed to be the exact same sort as their mother, from what Robert could tell. Not necessarily the insecurity, but the scheming and stratagems, to be sure. He didn't have enough information to judge the daughter, but Robert wasn't going to leave Lucy there to find out.

He thought of walking—he curbed the impulse to run—but realised Lucy would not thank him for making her walk home. She would consider it a social demotion to be sure. Young ladies did not walk about Town, she would say to him in that sad voice she knew would get to him whenever she tried it.

He arrived in the mews before the stable hands had untacked his curricle, so he was able to quickly climb up and set off, his mind racing far faster than he was able to travel on the crowded streets. Thankfully, his skill with the ribbons and his surefooted cattle got him through the mess at a reasonable speed, and he pulled up in front of the Bathurst townhouse within minutes of leaving his own.

A loitering urchin approached, and Robert tossed him a coin with the promise of another if he kept a close eye on his equipment. The child nodded and grinned, gazing up at Robert's horses in fascination while Robert bounded up the stairs and swung the knocker with vigour.

He was quickly shown into the salon and instantly caused a flutter of activity.

"Robert, what are you doing here?"

"What a pleasure to have you, my lord." Lucy and Lady Bathurst spoke over each other while the countess pulled a string that Robert assumed would summon servants. Whether they were to escort him from the premises or bring him tea, only time would tell, he thought with amusement.

Only Lady Isabelle remained silent and seated, watching him attentively with her wide, intelligent gaze and barely a glimmer of a smile.

With elevated eyebrows, Robert sat in an empty chair that had not been offered to him. He ignored the fact that he was being excessively rude. He didn't want his sister in these women's company despite his unignorable attraction to one of them.

"You didn't tell me you were going visiting this afternoon, Luce."

He spoke the words as gently as he could, but Robert was aware that everyone in the room knew they were intended as a rebuke.

Lucy valiantly tried to be defiant. "You said I could as long as I was accompanied."

"In reality, if I recall correctly, it was Lady Isabelle who advised you of the need for company. I didn't weigh in on the topic, but I expected you to show me the courtesy of keeping me apprised of your plans and locations. I doubt if this was a sudden decision or arrangement, so it is likely there would have been time to inform me. And that tells me that you hoped to keep me uninformed. Which does not sit well with me."

Lucy's eyes were growing rounder the longer he spoke, and to his regret, they began to fill with tears. Robert felt like a wretch, but he could not allow such behaviour to go unchecked. He could, however, wait until they were private to reprimand her further. He didn't know how to deal with tears. Since his own childhood and his mother's frequent weeping, he had never been able to tolerate the sight. And Lucy was no longer a toddler he could distract with sweets.

To his surprise and relief, Lady Isabelle handled the matter for him. He watched as she leaned over and grasped Lucy's hand.

"Don't get in a taking, pet. Your brother is worried for you, and that is as it should be. He knows you're still green and fresh from the country where everyone is your friend. If you didn't tell him where you were going, he was probably afraid for your safety. I'm certain he isn't angry with you, but men really hate to be frightened. So you probably ought to offer him an apology while we wait for the tea."

Robert did not wish to take tea with these people, but there was now nothing for it but to do so unless he wished to cause a scene that would be difficult to explain to his sister. Isabelle's words seemed to have worked miracles with Lucy. Her chuckle had been a little watery, but her tears had ceased. As if from thin air, Isabelle had produced a handkerchief for his sister to wipe her face with, and then she was all smiles as she offered him a pretty apology.

"I'm sorry, Robbie. I wanted to come so badly, and I knew you would be stuffy about my traipsing about Town, as you put it. I knew no harm could come to me if I was in Isabelle's company, so I didn't tell you."

Isabelle made a sound of distress, but didn't interrupt Lucy's apology. From the looks of things, Robert suspected the lady had not been in league with his sister for keeping a secret. Unless she was even more manipulative than he could fathom, and she had somehow convinced his sister to keep secrets without her knowing she was doing so.

Despite his recent suspicions that the young lady might be a foreign agent, he didn't think anyone was that wily or manipulative. He wasn't being needlessly naïve. Robert was well aware of just how twisted and skilled at manipulation some people could be, but he didn't think he was that easily duped, and he was convinced his sister was too clear-headed to fall for someone's tricks, even if it was a woman she was clearly idolising.

And that last thought was the one that gave him the most pause. His sister was under the young lady's influence, probably more than under his own. He would have to involve himself in Lucy's life even more than he'd expected if he was going to keep her safe. Perhaps Lady Bancroft's suggestion of helping him find a good school for her was one he ought to consider. He would discuss it with her once they were away from Lady Bathurst.

"Could I pour you a cup of tea, Lord Simmons?" Lady Bathurst asked in an annoyingly coy tone, setting Robert's teeth on edge and making him wish he had just grabbed Lucy and left immediately.

"Thank you, that would be lovely," was the only answer he could give. The way Isabelle hid her mouth behind her own cup and wouldn't meet his gaze told him she had noticed and found his predicament amusing, much to his irritation.

"Have you been here long, Lucy? It wouldn't do to overstay."

"Oh, no, I'm not doing that, am I?" Lucy turned to Isabelle with an anxiously beseeching expression.

"Not in the least," Isabelle replied immediately. "We have barely just gotten settled. I had thought we could go for a stroll or some other activity. You certainly haven't been longer than expected; have no fear."

"Oh, going for a stroll would be lovely."

The way she was looking at him from the corner of her eye told Robert how desperately she hoped he would change his mind about collecting her. Robert did his best to ignore the tug of emotion he couldn't avoid. He hated to be an ogre, but he couldn't very well leave his impressionable sister in this environment. *Am I being unforgivably unreasonable, though? What evidence do I have that the Bathursts are anything but what they appear to be—marriage-minded nobles doing what every other marriage-minded noble family had done for decades?*

Before he could respond to Lucy's hopes, though, Lady Bathurst started up a steady flow of social inanities that kept conversation moving while everyone sipped from their delicate cups. Robert participated out of ingrained habit, but he could see that Lucy was soaking in the experience with uninhibited delight. He tried not to sigh. The poor girl so clearly needed this sort of experience and education.

Should I allow her to stay? What harm could befall her? Surely Lady Bathurst wouldn't actually do anything to her. It was him she wanted. She would surely only wish to influence the girl in the way that would bring Robert to heel. If he was informed and prepared, surely he could counter her efforts. Until he found his viscountess, he needed female company for his sister. Appropriate female company. He couldn't decide if the Bathurst women fell into that category on one hand, but on the other, there were few more appropriate.

He couldn't help the small sigh that escaped him. The ever-attentive Lady Isabelle cast him a sharp, searching glance as though trying to read his thoughts. He could only hope she was incapable of such a feat. He knew his smile was weak, but he offered it to her anyway. One of her eyebrows quirked upward in a way that he refused to find attractive despite the lift it gave to his heart.

Ever since Bathurst and his family had turned up on his doorstep, Robert had been struggling to keep the beautiful young woman from his mind. Having her spend time with his sister was not going to help him with those efforts, he was well aware, but he couldn't deny his sister.

"Do make sure you are not out too late, Lucy."

The girl squealed, and while Lady Bathurst smiled indulgently and Isabelle stifled her amusement, Robert tried to hide his irritation at the sound. He had never realised that girls could make that sort of noise. He had so much to learn. Perhaps he should call on Lord Inglewood's daughter. What had Lady Bancroft said her name was? Carmen? Clarissa? Chloe?

He was out of his depth with his sister, and while he understood and acknowledged Lady

Bancroft's warning that choosing a wife for the sake of his nearly grown sister might not be for the best long-term solution for himself, he didn't see that he had any other choice. He couldn't very well allow Lucy to fall under the Bathurst influence no matter how much she might adore their daughter nor how lovely Robert found her.

Or he could send her away to school as was Lady Bancroft's other suggestion. But would Lucy feel that he had rejected her?

Robert gained his feet to take his leave. He had already acted foolishly enough for one day coming here as though he were on a mission to rescue his sister only to grant her permission to stay. He shook his head; what a bounder.

He bowed himself from the room with as much grace as he could muster while also trying not to appear as though he were running away although that was exactly what he was doing. He needed to use the time he had been granted to make inroads on his own project. Now that Bert and Lucy were living with him, he was going to have to manage his time even more carefully than he was used to. He may even need to leave his position at the Home Office.

It had been risky to take on the position in the first place when he didn't yet have a well-trained heir in place. Cuthbert wasn't ready to take his position as Viscount Simmons. Robert ought to ensure that he was never in that position. It was unkind to train up a spare who would never take over. That had been a stand Robert had shared with his father. With the vast age difference between Robert and his little brother, their father had thought it best not to even bother training the boy aside from the usual information any family member would be taught in order to generate familial pride. If the worst had happened, and both Robert and his father had been taken by the fever that killed the previous Lord Simmons, Bert was intelligent enough to be able to learn what was required. They had ensured the steward who helped run the estate was kind and hardworking. But the fever hadn't taken Robert, and he was now well ensconced as viscount himself. It was time that he ensure his lineage in a way that would not affect his brother, aside from being a doting uncle if he so chose.

Robert grinned as he climbed up into his curricle and tossed another coin to the urchin who had watched over his horses. The thought of his brother as an uncle was somehow stranger than the thought of him as a father.

He had never really thought about it, at least not consciously, but he supposed the arrival of his sister and brother when he was already fifteen years old had affected him greatly. He had felt protective of the infants rather than jealous of the new arrivals.

Robert's father had been delighted with their arrival even though he had never let on that he worried about having only Robert as heir. And he had never gone into any great detail about the rift that had kept his wife away from home for so many years and then brought her back again. Robert now knew it was his mother's scheming ways that had caused their troubles. But his father had ignored them for the sake of the young children. He had only once made any comment about it to Robert.

"I always regretted that you didn't have a mother. I couldn't let that happen to these two. I hope you understand."

Robert had nodded at the time although he hadn't really understood what his father was saying back then. He couldn't have known then that his mother's lavish attention was merely a manipulation.

Reliving those thoughts caused his stomach to clench, and he pushed them back down under the more urgent matters he needed to consider.

Chapter Fifteen

After Lord Simmons fairly scurried from the room, Belle and Lucy exchanged glances and giggles before Lady Bathurst shooed them from the house for the walk they had assured the viscount they wished to take. Belle collected her maid and the footman who had accompanied her earlier with the thought that she could accomplish multiple tasks at the same time.

"Do you always go about with multiple servants?" Lucy inquired, ever watchful of what she ought to imitate about her idol.

Belle fought embarrassment. "Not always. But in case we wish to stop in the shops, it would be good to have some assistance, don't you think?"

"Oh, yes, that's brilliant," the young girl exclaimed, making Belle struggle between amusement and chagrin over her deception of the girl.

The footman led the way, and they soon found themselves in the park Ellen had told Belle about earlier, where there was a good chance she might encounter Lord Hudson. Belle had second thoughts about involving Miss Lucretia in her research, but she couldn't see that there could possibly befall any harm to the girl, and it was all the better for her not to appear as though she were following the gentleman.

She wasn't following him, of course. In reality, she didn't know where the man was at the moment. It was just that there was a possibility of encountering him. She couldn't pass up that possibility. If she was to wed or at least become betrothed before the end of the Season, she had to use every possible opportunity.

She wasn't risking any harm to the girl, Belle insisted to herself even as guilt twisted in her stomach. She ought to be giving the younger girl her full attention rather than using her in her quest to find her match. Belle doubted Lord Simmons would appreciate her use of his sister if he were ever to discover it.

Belle was about to call off the entire excursion or perhaps alter it to take Lucy to Gunthers when the gentleman in question happened along.

"Why, Lady Isabelle, what a pleasant surprise," Lord Hudson called out as he doffed his hat and bowed before them.

To Belle's surprise, she blushed despite the fact that she had been expecting him. She nearly shook her head at her ridiculous reaction but managed not to blurt out anything that would embarrass her further. The worst of it was that she was not in the least bit fascinated by the gentleman. On paper he was perfect. But there was no spark such as she often felt in Viscount Simmons company. She wasn't sure if it was just her mixed-up feelings about having Lucy with her that was interfering with her enjoyment of the moment, but the man's thin face and crooked eyebrows, which had seemed somehow jaunty or dashing on previous viewing, now only seemed to suffer in comparison to Lord Simmons, her recently acquired scale of what was manly and handsome.

Belle ignored the swirling thoughts and emotions and pressed on with her intentions, dipping into a curtsy.

"It's a pleasure to come across you so unexpectedly, my lord," she said, hoping she didn't sound like a simpering ninny and almost rolling her eyes at nearly giving away her plan. Thankfully, the man didn't seem to notice.

"Who is your friend, my lady? I don't think we are acquainted," Lord Hudson asked, prompting Belle to perform the introductions.

"Simmons' sister?" Lord Hudson exclaimed in surprise, an odd expression flitting across his features. "I didn't know he had brought you to Town with him, my dear."

Lucy stared, shrugged, and smiled as though she wasn't certain what she ought to say to the man's declaration. "Are you good friends with my brother, my lord? I haven't spent a great deal of time with him of late, so I haven't heard him speak of his friends."

"Not great friends, I'll admit, but we do frequent the same club. I knew he had been out of Town for a time but hadn't heard that he was back."

"Oh yes, we returned the other day."

"So you came with him, then?"

"We all did," the girl replied ingeniously.

Belle realised that having Lucy along was the exact opposite of a brilliant plan. The implications would lead to disinterest on the part of Lord Hudson rather than her intention of possibly piquing his interest. Heat filled her cheeks.

"Would you believe we had carriage trouble on the way home from Everleigh?" Belle asked lightly. "We were fortunate that Lord Simmons came along and was able to help us get back to Town."

"That was fortuitous," Lord Hudson replied as his gaze shifted over her shoulder. The prickle Belle felt between her shoulders made her think it might be Lord Simmons. *Was the man everywhere?* She didn't dare turn to follow Lord Hudson's gaze to confirm. "My lord," Hudson hailed. "I didn't know you had taken your sister in. I trust all is well."

Belle sighed. It was just as she'd thought. Simmons must be following them to confirm that she wasn't getting up to nonsense with his sister. Would he think she was or she wasn't with this encounter, she wondered as she girded her courage and turned to face him. Her gaze encountered that of Lucy as she was turning, and the little darling was clearly delighted with her brother's arrival. For that reason only, Belle tried her best not to be disgruntled that he'd interrupted her efforts.

"Lord Simmons, what a surprise." Belle couldn't quite keep the dry note from her voice, but only the viscount seemed to notice if the uptick in the corner of his mouth was any indication.

"Good afternoon, I didn't think to encounter you lot here," he responded.

"We were just considering strolling over to Bond Street to look at ribbons," Belle said, ignoring her thought about ices at Gunther's. She didn't want either gentleman to think she was hinting for them to accompany them. She was far too embarrassed by the current encounter to be able to countenance the other, no matter her mother's directions to the contrary. She would undertake this effort on her own terms, not her mother's.

"Isn't Bond Street in the opposite direction from here?" Lord Simmons asked with a tightening of his gaze.

Belle forced a shrug. "We had thought to go to the park first and then realised we weren't in the appropriate disposition for scenery today." Belle held her breath, hoping Lucy didn't contradict her. They hadn't actually discussed their destination in the least aside from her explanation of why she had a maid and a footman with them.

Lucy blessedly remained quiet, merely watching the exchange with wide eyes as her head swiveled between each speaker. Lord Hudson seemed to be watching with amusement, as well, a fact Belle noted with far less relief. She didn't want to be the source of a gentleman's amusement. She wanted him to think her delightful and fascinating, not a good jest. She wanted to stamp her foot with frustration but curbed the impulse.

With a sigh, Belle accepted that this attempt at engaging with Lord Hudson had failed miserably. She wouldn't drag it out further. She turned to her young companion.

"What say you? To Bond Street for ribbons, then?"

Lucy still didn't speak but nodded her agreement vigorously.

Belle nodded to the two gentlemen in lieu of a farewell and turned her entourage around to stroll away. She sighed briefly to expel her disappointment, and then a puff of laughter surprised her.

"It would seem your brother is immensely concerned about you, doesn't it?"

Lucy grinned. "He is new to his role," the girl excused. "Well, not really as he has officially been our guardian ever since our father died, but he hasn't had us actually in his care before. I think he's having trouble realising I'm no longer an infant he has to watch over every minute.

Belle nodded in thought but then shook her head. "I think you're at far greater risk now that you're older than you would have been as a baby. This is why he's concerned about your whereabouts."

"What could possibly happen to me now? I am much bigger and have the ability to fend for myself."

Belle was a little dubious about this claim. "What can you truly do for yourself? You are growing up to be a beautiful young woman, and your speech, bearing, and attire proclaim that you are a *wealthy*, beautiful young woman. This would make you the target of any number of ne'er-do-wells. He is right to be concerned about you. Of course, since we told him you would be in my company, I am a trifle incensed that he remains concerned about you now."

Lucy shrugged, seeming not to notice that Belle wasn't jesting when she said she was irritated. "That's what older brothers do, isn't it? Don't yours do the same for you?"

"Not noticeably," she replied with a chuckle. "They are mostly too wrapped up with their own affairs to concern themselves with mine. But I'm also in the company of our parents, so I suppose they feel there is no need for them to trouble themselves with me. I do believe that if I required their assistance, I could ask for it. That is a comfort, to be sure." Just thinking of it brought a pang to her heart. She really ought to write to her brother and request his assistance under the circumstances. With their father still very much alive and in control of the family purse strings, though, Belle wasn't convinced there was anything her brother could do for her.

"Ladies."

Belle nearly jumped a foot in the air she was so startled by the sudden hail. This brought Lucy to a fit of the giggles. It took them both a moment to calm themselves enough to turn and stare at Lord

Simmons who had called to them. Belle was surprised she hadn't known he was near as she seemed to have a strange reaction whenever she found herself in his vicinity. He must need to be closer to have that effect on her, she mused even as she stared at him, waiting to find out what he would say about following them this time.

"My lord," she prompted when he said little.

"Might I have the pleasure of your company?" he asked as he climbed down from his curricle.

Belle looked at the high sporting vehicle. "I don't think we'll fit in that thing."

Simmons laughed. "I thought to walk with you."

"And just leave your horses here?" He surely must consider her truly dreadful company for his sister if he was willing to go to that risk, Belle thought with dismay.

Simmons shook his head with another chuckle. "Couldn't your footman escort them home for me? If I'm with you, you shan't need his assistance. If we buy too much, I'll hire a vehicle to bring you back."

Belle bit her lip in indecision. She didn't want to be in his strange company. His presence affected her equilibrium in distressing ways, and she couldn't remain focused on her task of finding an appropriate gentleman to wed. Lord Simmons didn't count. He obviously didn't trust her, and his presence would ward off other gentlemen, which was not her desired intention. But she couldn't very well send him away. Lucy wouldn't understand and would probably be frightfully disappointed.

There was nothing to do but nod and confer with her servants. Ellen would remain, but the footman would drive the viscount's pair of horses and his fine curricle back to his mews. It was evident the young man was delighted by the prospect.

"Have you driven a pair before?" Suddenly Simmons sounded as though he realised he might have made a mistake. Belle had to bite her lip anew to control her amusement.

"Oh, yes, m'lord. I've trained in the stables at Bathurst when the family hasn't needed me in the house. I swear I'll be ever so careful."

Belle frowned at Lord Simmons. It had been his idea. He shouldn't now be making her footman embarrassed or afraid.

Simmons met and searched Belle's gaze, making her belly flutter and tumble in an almost delicious manner. How perfectly ridiculous. She lifted her eyebrows at him, and he grinned.

"Very well, Thomas, I'm sorry for having doubted you for a moment," Simmons said, when he'd finally torn his gaze from Belle's. "I appreciate your allowing me to take your more important task from you."

Thomas grinned, not agreeing in the least that he had received the lesser assignment. The footman bobbed a bow to his mistress and then carried on his way without a glance back, evidently delighted with the turn of events.

Belle watched him go. “I suppose I ought to speak to my father about allowing Thomas to change his assignment to that of groom or stable hand.”

“That would surely be a demotion, wouldn’t it?”

Belle frowned. “It doesn’t seem Thomas thinks so.”

Robert stared at her for a moment and then one half of his mouth lifted in a sort of half-smile that twisted her stomach into a flutter. Belle could only stare back at him, hoping she didn’t look like a gaping fish. For the briefest moment, she felt as though she were leaning toward him, that if she could only put her head on his shoulder for a moment, or have him hold her in his clearly strong arms, she would be able to solve all of her life’s dilemmas.

She blinked and stepped back. What an odd thing to think and feel. Heat crept into her cheeks, and she turned to Lucy in an attempt to break the strange hold the viscount had on her. Belle cleared her throat delicately and smiled at her young friend.

“What do you think? Is his lordship any good at matching colours?”

It didn’t seem as though Lucy had noticed the momentary fascination the two adults had with each other, much to Belle’s relief. She still felt as though she could barely breathe, so tight had been the constriction in her chest for a brief period. The strangest part was that it had been thrilling rather than scary. She needed to get away from Simmons, which meant she would have to reject the girl. It was a pity. But Belle refused to moon over a man who was determined to curb her influence on his sister.

Chapter Sixteen

Robert didn't know what had just happened. One minute, he's on his way home, satisfied that no harm will come to his sister even if he doesn't trust the lady she's with. The next, after encountering said lady rendezvousing with a known foreign agent, he finds himself offering to escort them to shop for, what had she said? Ribbons? He knew himself for a fool. A part of him wanted to arrest the lot of them, his sister included. He certainly couldn't leave Lucy in Lady Isabelle's questionable influence. *Why was the woman and her servants encountering the traitorous Lord Hudson?* That was the question he needed to get to the bottom of. But he couldn't have Lucy in the middle while he did so.

He ought to be getting on with his own necessary things, including the investigation into Lord Hudson. With Bert and Lucy staying with him, he didn't have nearly the free time or circumstances that he'd once had. It was likely he would have to step away from his role with the Home Office. That was a disappointment, but he was prepared to make such a change for his siblings' sake.

Perhaps, though, if he were to find himself a wife, he wouldn't have to make such a sacrifice. Of course, a wife was likely to want his time and attention at least at times, but it shouldn't interfere nearly so much with his attention and concentration as worrying about Lucy and Bert was doing.

But then he thought about the strange sensations he experienced whenever he was in the company of Lady Isabelle, and he suspected he was being rather foolish to think a wife would be less consuming. If a young woman he didn't even like nor trust could affect him in such a way, how would his wife change his life?

Perhaps he ought to reconsider the matter. There was still the possibility of sending Lucy away to school. Robert gave his head a shake and brought his attention back to the far more urgent matter of Lady Isabelle's influence over his sister.

The fact that he found the beautiful young woman an attractive distraction was evidence enough that he had nearly lost his mind. The woman was clearly up to no good. Was she using his sister in some sort of plot? Did it have to do with the government? Or was she just trying to entrap him privately?

Robert's attraction to the woman felt like an act of disloyalty to the Crown given his suspicions. Perhaps that in itself disqualified him from his position with the Office.

The girls were talking about ribbons.

Could she really be a treasonous agent if she could walk along the street, arm in arm with a half-grown girl, talking about the best places to buy hair ties? He supposed in his years with the Office he had seen stranger things, but this would be one of the strangest, he was certain. Perhaps he ought to discuss the matter over with Lord Chamberlain.

Robert resolved to do so at his first opportunity. In the meantime, he had to make sure his sister was cared for.

“Of course, I am excellent at matching colours,” he spoke up from behind the two females before him. He stepped closer, in between them, and offered them each one of his elbows. “Shall we stroll?” he asked gallantly with a bit of a flourish, ignoring the tingles that shot through his arm when Isabelle placed her small hand into the crook of his arm. She wasn’t much bigger than his sister, but the sensations were far different. Again, he was swept with conflicting feelings of attraction and a sense that he was betraying his country or some such dramatic thing.

Robert forced himself to relax and remain as he was. She was just a small, young woman. There was very little damage she could manage to do while right under his nose. Until he could get to the bottom of the situation with her, as to whether or not she truly was an agent or just the unfortunate daughter of scheming parents, he would keep her where he could watch her.

To his immense surprise, the afternoon flew by. The laughter his sister shared with the young woman she clearly idolised was heartwarming to the solitary man who had kept to himself too much in the decade since he had inherited his title. To his further surprise, he had truly enjoyed the very feminine task of sorting through ribbons and selecting the exact perfect shades for whatever the girls had in mind.

He couldn't fathom what they wanted all the scraps of fabric for, and he had lied when he said he could sort the shades, but they seemed not to notice, and he found it fascinating that they could insist there was much difference between this blue and the other blue. Robert merely shrugged and watched in amusement as they debated the perfect texture of string for holding back their locks.

"Especially when one is at home, it's comfortable to have a looser style that's just tied back with a ribbon, wouldn't you agree?" Isabelle asked Lucy artlessly. "One grows quite tired of having pins jabbed into your head every night."

"Never say so, my lady," Lucy breathed. "It is one of the things I am most looking forward to."

Isabelle's laughter did strange things to Robert's equilibrium for a moment, and he almost missed what she said next.

"I trust you mean you are looking forward to putting your hair up and going out, not the actual act of having all the pins jabbed at you."

Lucy giggled. "I am willing to put up with the minor inconvenience for the immense pleasure I anticipate gaining when I am finally allowed to go about Society."

"Oh, my dear, I do hope it turns out to be the delight you are expecting."

Lucy didn't seem to notice but Robert heard the note of regret in Isabelle's voice. He wondered what put it there. Was she jaded by her one Season already? Or was it more nefarious than that? Had she been forced into whatever scheming traits she was caught up in?

Robert didn't want to find sympathy for someone he thought might be in league with traitors, but he couldn't help softening further toward the lovely woman.

It was more than obvious to Robert that Lucy would be safe in Lady Isabelle's company at least for the time being. Even though he had found them in the company of Lord Hudson, Robert expected that his sister's youth and innocence would protect her from even realising anything was amiss. He would be better off asking at the Office if they knew anything about Lord Bathurst or his youngest daughter.

He took his leave of them after paying for their selections.

Pink tinged Isabelle's cheeks becomingly as she tried to refuse his gift. "I have my pin money, my lord; you needn't treat me."

"It's such a small thing, my lady, and it gives me pleasure. Don't take that away from me just for your scruples."

Robert saw that she wasn't sure how to respond. The confused blinking and puzzled expression would have been endearing if he wasn't trying so hard to be indifferent to her.

"I will see you for supper, Luce," Robert called as he waved them off even as he regretted sending his curricle home with the footman. He ought to have kept it, he thought before dismissing the concern. He would likely be able to make better time on his own two feet anyway. He put the ladies into a hackney before taking his leave of them.

Robert made his way to the back door of the nondescript building down a side street near the better-known government offices. His department of the Home Office wasn't exactly a secret, but an attempt was always made to be as discreet as possible. His involvement, of course, *was* more of a secret. As a noble, he would be an even bigger target than a regular agent, so it was best to keep his involvement quiet. Besides, it was far easier to find things out if he was merely thought to be a meddlesome viscount rather than an investigative agent for the Crown.

"Lord Chamberlain will see you now, my lord," the thin young man currently clerking for their chief agent announced.

"Simmons, this is a"—the older man hesitated as though searching for the perfect word—"surprise."

Robert never showed up unannounced. Lord Chamberlain hated surprises. But it couldn't be helped.

"Thank you for seeing me without a scheduled appointment, sir. I have had a change of circumstances I thought I ought to tell you about. And those changed circumstances affect my schedule, making it a challenge to meet appointments."

"Now I'm intrigued. Have you finally found your viscountess?"

Robert laughed. "No, sir. My brother and sister have just moved in with me."

"I see," the older man replied. "Are you here to tell me you must leave your service to His Majesty?"

"Not at this time, sir. I am merely keeping you informed of my change. But I also have a different matter I'd like to ask you about, if I may be so bold as to make a claim on your time."

"Don't be namby-pamby, Simmons; of course you can ask my advice or whatever else you have buzzing in your bonnet."

Robert laughed, as was likely the intention, over the man's wording.

"As you know, I've been looking into Lord Hudson and the suspicions of his being a foreign agent involved in the plots we've been investigating. I can't prove it yet, but I know he's involved in that failed attempt to kidnap His Majesty. And I have reason to believe Lord Bathurst's daughter, Lady Isabelle, is investigating him, as well. Is she connected with this department?"

"A gently bred female, Simmons, really?"

Robert shrugged. "I was of the opinion there was no limit to the lengths you will go to protect the nation."

"That may well be true, my boy, but there are enough women in the world that I have never yet needed to involve a noblewoman."

"So you don't have any knowledge of her being an agent of any sort?"

Lord Chamberlain looked down his lean nose at his visitor, making Robert feel like a recalcitrant schoolboy. "I know that Lady Isabelle is just about the sweetest young woman I've had the pleasure of meeting. Her father is an odd fellow, and her mother seems to have suddenly decided to quit all responsibilities, but before they lost their minds, they managed to raise six quite decent children."

"What do you mean Lady Bathurst has quit all responsibilities?" Robert was always amazed at the older gentleman's bounty of information. He didn't think there was a single activity or even a thought that took place without Chamberlain's knowledge.

"According to my sources, and even what the lady herself has said in my hearing, she doesn't want to escort the girl about Town. Wants to wed her off as quickly as possible. It is the strangest development I've seen in a family. There doesn't seem to be any real concrete reason behind it that we can tell. They haven't lost their money; there aren't any health crises. They just don't want to be responsible for their children anymore. And the earl is making odd speeches in the House. It's possible he *has* lost his mind. I cannot say for certain as he was always a trifle odd in his viewpoints. But Lady Bathurst is determined her daughter is to wed immediately."

"And they don't seem to mind to whom?"

"Well, they aren't sending her off with one of the footmen if that's what you're asking."

Robert sighed and told his boss his suspicions about their carriage trouble on his doorstep. To his surprise, the chief agent laughed.

"They're far wilier than I would have expected. Perhaps there's nothing actually wrong with Bathurst, after all. Good for them. It would be a good match for both of you, so there's no need to cut up over it. It isn't as though they tried to trick you into a bad match."

"I have no desire to be tricked into any match, my lord," Robert countered stiffly.

"You have to wed someone."

Robert was rather offended at the man's *laissez faire* attitude about his own personal future. Arguing with his overseer about the matter wasn't going to improve the situation so he chose to drop the subject and concentrate on the other reason he had stopped by.

"So, as far as you know, there is no reason to suspect Lady Isabelle is an agent for us or for any other agency?"

"That sweet young woman might be smart enough to be one, but no, she is an innocent lady out looking for a husband."

"Well, in that case, then, she might be considering Lord Hudson as her match."

"Lord Hudson? Good heavens, why? What makes you think that?"

Robert proceeded to tell Lord Chamberlain all about their encounter in addition to what he had witnessed of her two servants following the traitorous agent.

Lord Chamberlain sighed. "I should have made sure he was expelled from Society before now. Of course he's considered eligible, Simmons. He's just like you on the surface. Young, handsome, rich, and titled. Why wouldn't she consider him a match?"

"The bounder is conspiring against His Majesty," Robert burst out.

"That's true. But it didn't make him sprout horns and a tail, so there is no warning for the innocent who don't know to look for the things we see."

Robert didn't want to accept Lord Chamberlain's words. If one was so innocent, shouldn't they be able to sense the wickedness in others? He didn't for a second believe Lady Isabelle was completely innocent. She must be guilty of something, he thought. And he had left his sweet, young sister in her company. With a shake of his head he realised he was the idiot this time and bowed himself out of Lord Chamberlain's presence.

He would have to find Lucy and protect her from Lady Isabelle himself. Whether she was innocent of government intrigue or not, Robert didn't believe the young noblewoman was completely innocent. Even if it was just thinking Lord Hudson would make a good match, that at least revealed exceptionally poor judgement on her part, thus marking her as a poor companion for his impressionable young sister.

Chapter Seventeen

After a week of *ton* activities, Isabelle was starting to feel ragged. She had been to as many balls, routs, musicales, and suppers as she could manage to squeeze into a se'en-night, but she was no closer to her goal of finding a husband who would truly want her for herself or even her dowry, for that matter. She had done too good a job of portraying her disinterest early in the Season, it would seem. Of course, there were a couple of gentlemen who were starting to appear more interested, but Belle had vowed to herself she would not set her cap at anyone.

It was a fine line she was treading, trying to balance not appearing too eager and yet no longer being standoffish. But it was finally starting to work. There were three gentlemen towering over her in the parlor at that very moment. It was just too bad that none of them really interested her in an appreciable way. Perhaps if they truly started to pursue her with any degree of enthusiasm, she would warm up to them considerably.

And the fact that they did not measure up to the standard her obstinate mind had decided upon was neither here nor there. Lord Simmons was not for her, she reminded herself for the tenth time that morning. He would not be calling upon her. It was evident to her if not to everyone else that he had taken her in dislike. He tolerated his sister's adoration of her just barely enough to permit them to stroll in the park now and again. But he was not one of her admirers.

And that was perfectly fine, Belle repeated in her mind even as she smiled and nodded at something Lord Hudson was saying.

Perhaps a week hadn't yet been long enough, she thought to herself in a soothing tone. Even her inner thoughts were trying to calm her. She must surely be losing her mind. Over a gentleman. It couldn't be borne. She had promised herself she would never lose her mind over any man at a young age. One of her sisters had constantly been losing her mind over whichever new male she'd encountered. She had only been thirteen years old when she had assured herself that would never be her. About Lucy's age.

And now her thoughts were back to circling around Lord Simmons.

Belle almost sighed aloud but managed to keep her restless thoughts to herself even as she despaired that she wouldn't find a husband before her parents decided to cast her from their home.

Could they truly do that?

Belle didn't believe they abhorred her. They were simply done with being parents. It was an odd development. She hadn't asked to be born. But with six children spread over many years, Belle supposed it had begun to lose its attraction for them. Still, it wasn't her fault, and she rather resented their decision to be finished before the task was actually concluded.

Perhaps she could confront them about it rather than running herself ragged in the pursuit of fulfilling their request.

No, she would rather wed. She had to do so anyway; there was no reason to resist.

Another sigh threatened just as Lord Hudson was leaning closer to make a point. What was he talking about? A moment of panic threatened her equilibrium, but she managed to pull her thoughts together and return to the matter at hand. He was spouting some nonsense about a tidbit of gossip that everyone had been talking of for days. Nothing that required much thought on her part. She was able to laugh in the appropriate spot despite her dismay over the foolish topic.

Gossip was really a waste of time. Why could he not be discussing the latest play or a book he'd read, or even something taking place in the news sheets?

Lord Simmons would know what was taking place in the world, she was certain.

"Lord Simmons to see you, my lady."

Belle nearly fell out of her chair, she was so surprised by the butler's announcement. She had thought the man would never call. He had made it clear he didn't approve of her.

When she'd encountered him at the theatre four nights past, he had nearly given her the cut direct. His nod had been the barest acknowledgement of their acquaintance, and he had avoided eye contact with her. It had made her breath catch in the back of her throat, but she followed his suit and averted her gaze without even returning his nod.

When she had seen him at the Northumberland ball, he had avoided making eye contact with her when it was evident she didn't have a partner for the next dance. This one had slightly embarrassed her as she felt like a wallflower for the first time in her life. Their hostess had quickly clucked over her and introduced her to a rather awkward gentleman just up from the country, and the evening had progressed as though nothing had happened. But Isabelle had begun counting the injuries. It was unlike her to hold a grudge, but this was outside of enough.

When she had been seated near him at the Rose Park supper, he had managed to converse with everyone except her. Belle had felt the sting of his ignoring her as though he had slapped her. Colour stained her cheeks for the entire evening as mortification festered in her soul. The partners she had available to her for conversation were neither well read nor the least bit interesting, unlike Viscount Simmons. Belle had seen his library. She knew the titles there and was well aware they were not merely for display. Each and every one of them had been well worn, indicating much use. Belle had thought, at the time, that she would very much enjoy discussing them with his lordship. If they were friends, that was. Clearly they were not.

And no one had noticed but her.

That was the feat she found most surprising. With Society's penchant and thirst for gossip, it was the biggest shock that their names weren't on everyone's tongues. But it seemed to Belle that no one but her was aware that Lord Simmons never acknowledged her.

So why had he called?

"Is Lucy well?" Belle blurted, the sudden concern making her speak before she had completely thought the matter through.

"Of course, why do you ask?" The viscount frowned as though she might know something he didn't.

"I was surprised to see you," she muttered, grateful that the other occupants of the room had stepped back to allow Simmons to greet her. To her further surprise, he laughed.

She had thought he was too serious and somber to do something so frivolous as laugh in her company.

"She is well as far as I know. I called to ask you if you went to school."

Belle blinked at him. They were in a salon full of fashionable people, and he was asking her a rather pedantic question.

"School?" she asked, uncaring that she sounded like a ninny, repeating his last word.

"Yes, my lady. Did you go to school or were you only instructed by governesses?"

"There is a lovely school for ladies very close to Bathurst. I had the opportunity to attend as a day student. It was lovely." She knew she was repeating herself, but she was still a little scrambled from her surprise at seeing him.

"Does that school also take boarders?"

Belle smiled when what she wanted to do was frown. "Are you sure everything is fine with your sister? Can I do anything to assist her? Or you?" she added at the end.

"You can answer my questions," he all but growled at her.

Heat flushed her face, but a quick sweep of the room from beneath her eyelashes showed her that no one was overtly paying them any attention. That didn't completely calm her anxious thoughts because she was well aware that most members of the ton were well able to eavesdrop without appearing to do so.

Belle's chin rose in defiance. This "gentleman" had been nearly giving her the cut direct for a week and now he was interrogating her about which school she attended? This was outside of enough.

"You would be better off asking ladies whom you like or at least respect for their recommendations for schools if you're thinking to send Miss Lucretia away. The school I attended was quite lovely, but I cannot say what the boarding experience was like, nor would I expect you to appreciate my recommendation. I'm sure you'd be more comfortable speaking with Lady Chloe, but I am not certain that she actually went away to school either."

Belle gestured for a footman to approach and turned back to Lord Simmons. "If we can offer you any refreshments, please let one of the footmen assist you."

And then she turned back to the gentlemen she had been conversing with, unconcerned that she had returned rudeness to the viscount's own rudeness. It was unlike her, but she also was determined not to have her feelings injured any further by the handsome dolt of a man.

Chapter Eighteen

Robert's chin threatened to become unhinged from his shock. The lady had more of a backbone than he would have expected. And her concern for his sister was obviously genuine. He could see it in her eyes. He truly believed the young woman to be guileless. Even when up close and able to stare straight into her expressive eyes, he couldn't see any deceit in her. Aside from the usual attempt not to be overheard or gossiped about but that was pedestrian and average for any member of society, he would expect—not something he ought to judge her for. In fact, he himself was far more clandestine and secretive than Lady Isabelle ever proved to be.

And yet he still avoided her as though she had the plague. Until today, when he hadn't been able take his concerns of his sister any longer and sought her out in a fit of indecision. And she had returned his own behaviour back upon him. How embarrassing.

But even in a fit of pique, she was kindness itself, Robert realised. She had been quiet and circumspect, not yelling or creating a scene, even providing an offer of refreshments and an implied invitation to remain and enjoy the Bathurst hospitality, such that it was, if what he had learned from Lord Chamberlain was true.

Of course, Robert never questioned Lord Chamberlain's information. Perhaps he would have to begin to question his wisdom in one area of his life. The man had, in actual fact, suggested that Lady Isabelle might be a good match for him despite Robert's suspicions about her and his aversion to her parents' scheming ways.

It was for that reason that he had so aggressively avoided her ever since. In hindsight, he had probably been unforgivably rude to her. Unkind even. Not that she was really in a precarious social situation. She was well connected, beautiful, and reputed to have a generous dowry. It was strange that she wasn't yet betrothed if it was true that her parents were anxious to have her off their hands.

Robert's suspicious nature couldn't settle itself in connection with her. There was obviously more to the situation than met the eye. He didn't think it was possible that Lord Chamberlain could be wrong on a topic, but Robert was certainly not going to place his future and that of his family in such a precarious situation.

It had been a foolish impulse to come here. Lady Isabelle was not for him, he reminded himself for the hundredth time. And she didn't have useful advice to assist him with his sister. He ought to carry on with his own affairs.

But worrying about Lucy and even Bert was interfering with those affairs. He ought to have found the evidence against Hudson already. That bounder ought to have been on the last boat destined for Botany Bay. Instead, Simmons was in Lady Isabelle's receiving room along with a horde of others.

That lowering thought spurred him from the room. What a waste of his time this call had been. After an appropriate length of time so as not to draw attention to it, he quietly took his leave.

And still, though, as he drove away, Robert couldn't help remembering how pretty Isabelle looked as she welcomed him in her floaty pink frock. He had no idea what sort of fabric it was or what you would call the style, but it seemed as though she moved in a cloud, like a creature from a dream.

He was being beyond ridiculous. A creature from a nightmare would be more accurate, he reminded himself, ignoring the sparks and tingles he experienced whenever he was nearby that particular woman. Perhaps he ought to actively remember those strange reactions. Surely being struck by lightening on a regular basis would not be a comfortable way to live. He didn't want sparks in his life. He wanted a comfortable home and a safe place for his siblings and children.

But didn't he want a family of his own? A happy, interesting family? A joy-filled one as Lady Isabelle had once mentioned? Perhaps sparks were a good thing?

Robert growled low in his throat and shook his head even as he guided his horses through the busy street. He didn't have time for nonsensical thoughts. The future would have to sort itself. Right now, he had Lucy and Bert to consider. Cuthbert needed to be in school, but that sweet lad was too concerned about his sister to leave and was thus losing an entire year of school. Before long, the term would be finished so unless Rob wanted to send his brother to a nearly empty school for the summer term, which would be barely productive for the boy, he would have to keep him home until the fall term started.

That would be a good time to send Lucy to some sort of school, as well.

He should have thought of all this before he went haring about all over Town trying to find answers to every single one of his questions. Of course, place would be made for his sister wherever he chose to send her. He wasn't being overly high in the instep to think that. He was certain the girl was smart enough and perfectly acceptable. Any school would be happy to have her whether he gave a generous donation or not.

But if he found the perfect school and they tried to tell him they were full, he knew exactly how to get his sister in the door.

That might not spell success for the girl, though. Robert sighed. Despite the time he knew he had gained for himself by realising he had a few months to get it all figured out, there were still so many factors, and feelings, he knew nothing about. He still needed a wife. And as soon as possible.

But that too would have to wait.

Lord Hudson was now a more urgent matter than Robert's home or family situation. If the man was indeed behind the latest plot to upend the government, Robert needed to find the evidence and have the man expelled from the country.

Robert was of the mind that deportation was too good for traitors, but even the king, who was often the target of these sorts of plots, was soft on the noblemen who might be so "misguided." Robert didn't think it mere misdirection of a fully grown noble. Any man who wished to harm his own country and its king wasn't truly a man and certainly couldn't be considered noble by any stretch of the imagination or whichever definition of the word you might consider.

And yet that is what Hudson faced. A long ride on an uncomfortable ship and a new life far from home if he survived the passage.

If Robert could find the evidence he knew must exist. If he could get his mind fully engaged on the matter. Robert knew he ought to engage the assistance of some other agents considering how lacking in wits he had become in the last se'en-night, but Lord Chamberlain thought it best to keep the fewest people possible informed on the subject.

Lord Hudson had a great number of friends. Even within the Office, it couldn't be completely relied upon that information wouldn't escape into the wrong hands. This thought troubled Robert the most. He couldn't fully trust the ones he most had to rely upon. It was a disheartening and disconcerting fact.

Bracing himself, Simmons set about concluding his investigation. He would have to deal with his worries about Lucy and Bert later.

Chapter Nineteen

Despite Viscount Simmons evident low opinion of her, Isabelle hadn't stayed away from his sister. She had considered it, to be perfectly honest, but she hadn't been able to bring herself to abandon the girl. Whenever they spoke, Lucy seemed perfectly content with her lot living with her brother, especially if it also meant she could spend time, on occasion, with her mentor, the lovely Lady Isabelle.

It took great effort on Belle's part not to roll her eyes in embarrassment and exasperation whenever the girl gushed in praise of her, but she hadn't yet been able to curb Lucy's impulse to do so at too frequent intervals. She might not want to listen to praise of herself, but Belle was happy to listen when the girl described how her brother was directing her life.

They were strolling down the street, with no real direction in mind, Ellen following them at a slight distance, as Lucy described her latest art projects.

"I know you have been too busy to call by, but you really must visit me at my house, or rather

Robbie's house, I suppose. Would that not be seemly? Or I could even just bring it down to the foyer to show you when you call to collect me if you won't stay for a visit."

Belle laughed. "Wouldn't that be difficult? How big is your frame?"

"Oh, I couldn't tell you that. It's not exceptionally large, as far as paintings go. But even if it's too ungainly for me, one of the footmen would be sure to help. And I want you to see it. I don't mean to be overly boastful, but even I can see that my skill is improving."

"What do you think has made the difference? Have you hired a tutor?"

"Oh no," the girl scoffed, "nothing so organised as all that. Robbie said he would get one for me if I wished, but he suggested practice might be all I need."

"Is your brother turning into a nipfarthing on you?" Belle asked with a laugh.

"Not at all. But I think he is actually afraid I will develop a *tendre* for any tutor he hires."

Belle laughed again. "I can see how that is a risk you run at your age."

"Did you fall in love easily when you were my age?"

Belle sobered, realising this was not the light subject she had first meant it to be. "I didn't, but one of my sisters did. It caused a great deal of drama in my family and taught me not to be so quick to give my heart away."

Lucy's eyes were huge as she gazed up at Belle, eager for more information. It was the strangest sensation to Belle. In the midst of her increasingly desperate search for a husband, she enjoyed her interludes with the younger girl. In some ways, she found it motivational to finding a husband. Perhaps having children could be a similar experience to the relationship she had developed with Lucy.

Belle shook her head. Her relationship with Lucy was not one of mother and daughter. It was much more like sisters or what she thought a big-sister-little-sister relationship could be although she hadn't necessarily had this type of bond with her own sisters. Whatever the case, she enjoyed the girl and hoped Simmons wouldn't finally put an end to their association.

She dragged her attention back to the conversation at hand.

"It is a reasonable concern your brother is showing, although it might be possible for him to find a female artist to give you some instruction if you thought you might benefit from some guidance. But I think his lordship is correct—often with art, it's practice and experimentation that helps you to improve, rather than instruction from someone else after you've learned the basics."

"But what sort of drama resulted with your sister?"

Lucy's impatient question caused more laughter from Belle. "For one thing, the household went through a good number of tutors for a while as my father would have to send them off whenever my sister's feelings got the better of her. Which always struck me as unfair. It wasn't the tutor's fault she was such a mad thing."

"Was she compromised?" Lucy asked, sounding both scandalised and intensely curious, making Belle snort.

"No!" she answered immediately. "It never got so out of hand. I rather think the poor tutors were relieved to be sent away as she was no doubt a great irritant to them, aside from their loss of income. All I meant to say was your brother wasn't necessarily being ungenerous to not wish to hire you a tutor."

"Oh," Lucy countered, "I never suspected he was. I think he merely doesn't know what to do with me now that I've settled myself into his household. I'm not an infant, nor an adult, and I've never gone to school, so I'm a bit stuck in the middle of circumstances."

It suddenly occurred to Belle that they were heading toward the park where they had encountered Lord Hudson days earlier, and she became uncomfortable at the thought of taking her young companion there again. How had she managed to inadvertently choose a destination? It struck her as odd that Lucy might have chosen the direction.

"Do you have somewhere in particular in mind where we are going?" Belle asked after a moment.

"I thought you particularly liked the park we strolled in the other day, where we encountered Robbie and his friend."

“Can you believe that was only my second or third time there?” Belle asked with laughter that sounded a little forced. “Perhaps we ought to find our way to Hyde Park or Gunthers or even the shopping district.”

Lucy shrugged. “I haven’t any particular plans for today; I just wanted to have a visit with you.”

Isabelle’s heart melted a little from this declaration. “That’s the nicest compliment I’ve yet received, Lucy, thank you. I truly enjoy spending time with you, as well.” A glance farther along showed they were nearly at the park. She shrugged mentally. What harm could it do? “You will find it is quite a lovely spot, not overcrowded or noisy. I do enjoy getting a break from the noise of city life sometimes.”

Lucy’s smile widened. “I haven’t become tired of the noise yet, but Robbie assures me that I will.”

Belle laughed. “Does his lordship mind that you call him by such a moniker?”

Lucy wrinkled her nose. “Do you think he might? I’ve been calling him that since I learned to talk. It never occurred to me that I should call him something else.” She frowned at Isabelle. “Are you formal with your family? Even Mother doesn’t get starchy very often, and she can be a stickler about some things.”

“My family can be very formal upon occasion. We have been calling my brother by his courtesy title since he was born, I think. That is almost all I’ve ever called him. I sometimes forget he has other names.”

Lucy's face appeared puzzled. "I suppose it's just a name, but don't you find that it puts distance between you? Like you can't really be friends if you have to be honouring him all the time?"

"You make an interesting point, Lucy. Is that why you never call me by name? You want to be friends, but you don't want to appear rude so you just don't call me anything?"

Lucy laughed. "I don't think I did it consciously but that does sound like a good explanation. Would you prefer I be more formal?"

Belle squeezed the girl's hand where it was tucked into her elbow as they strolled along the quiet street into the park.

"Not in the least, my young friend. I told you before, I've always wanted a little sister. I don't think I would ever be formal with her, so that would be you. Let's not be formal when we're just the two of us. In company, of course, we have to do what is accepted. But I would be honoured if you would call me Belle. Almost no one does, but it's what I think of as my given name."

"Very well, Belle. I like it," the girl answered immediately, a wide smile returning to her face. "And you already call me Lucy, so we are comfortable."

"What do your brothers call you?"

"Bert always calls me Lucy or Luce. Robbie changes what he calls me depending on the circumstances. He isn't so formal most of the time, but he does often call me Lucretia, my full name, especially if he's deep in thought or cross with me."

Belle laughed. "Is he often cross with you?"

Lucy laughed, too. "Not very often. It's more likely for him to be deep in thought on a matter. He has so many serious things to think about. I don't know how he manages it all. I would surely lose track of all the responsibilities he has to keep in his head." She suddenly sobered. "I probably ought to be sorry that we have pushed ourselves upon him, but he is our family, and I just couldn't bear it with our mother and her husband any longer."

"I am certain your brother was thrilled to have you join his household. Do not fret about that."

Lucy eyed her askance. "That is a trifle too enthusiastic, Belle," she said dryly, causing a giggle to erupt from Isabelle's throat just as she spotted the very subject of their conversation across the green expanse before them.

The giggle died in her throat as she wondered what he could possibly be doing, finding them there in that park once more. The way he held so watchful and still struck Belle as strange, and a frown began to form on her forehead as her gaze followed his to see that he almost appeared to be staring at Lord Hudson. How very irregular, she thought before her thoughts were interrupted by Lucy.

The young girl who had seemed to be showing such signs of maturity had followed Isabelle's gaze and caught sight of her brother. Suddenly, her few years were evident as she scampered toward him, shouting his name before Belle could catch her back.

It was hard to interpret the expression on the viscount's face from a distance, but Isabelle was certain they had interrupted something important. What that was, she couldn't begin to fathom, but she hurried forward to try to mitigate the disaster.

Everything was a bit of a blur after that. Seemingly out of nowhere, several men bounded forward, between Lucy and Lord Simmons, blocking the girl's way as they hurried toward Lord Hudson, seeming to tackle him to the ground.

Lucy was so stunned by the development, she stood still and gaped, allowing Isabelle to catch up to her and pull her into the limited security of her arms while Lord Simmons shot them a vile glare, but after a brief hesitation, he followed after the other men. Within seconds that felt like hours to Belle and likely Lucy, as well, Lord Hudson was being bundled into a secure coach along with at least four other mean-looking men, and they all disappeared, leaving Lord Simmons to stare after them longingly for a second before he strode forward to confront the females.

Isabelle had stood frozen with Lucy in her arms as the entire scene had unfolded. It had felt for a moment as though it were a very dramatic spectacle on a stage or a bad dream but Lucy's trembling and her own—she added the mental thought—assured her that it was a very real situation.

"What are you two ninnies doing here? You could have jeopardised the entire mission. Or you could have been irreparably injured. How foolish could you be? I told you not to leave the house," he ranted at Lucy before turning to Belle. "And I thought my feelings had been made clear to you. Are you too thick in the head to take a hint?"

The shock of it all had slowed Belle's wits, and for a moment, she could only blink at the viscount while tears threatened to humiliate her, but then she pulled herself together, keeping her arms around the man's sister but gathering her dignity close and standing at her highest height. It might only bring her to a level with his shoulders, but it made her feel better about herself not to be cowering before him. She spoke with as much calm as she could muster and only prayed her voice wouldn't tremble as she told Lord Simmons exactly what she thought of him.

"We are good and decent ladies who have no idea what just happened here or what you have involved yourself in. We happened to be out for a stroll. And while, yes, your lack of feeling towards me has been very evident, you did not forbid me your sister's company. Since she hasn't yet been presented to anyone and you have been busy with your own affairs, she has been in need of company, and we were both in need of air. It was the worst of unfortunate coincidences that had our paths crossing yours this afternoon. If you had some sort of questionable business to perform, you should have ensured it was done somewhere else, far from others. If it wasn't us who happened by, it could have been anyone else. You should count yourself fortunate that it was us rather than Lady Jersey or one of her friends. We shan't bruit this about town as some might.

She had to take a deep breath to stem the rising flow of her words but managed to add one final thought. "I will see Lucy home and then I hope to never lay eyes upon you again in my entire life, which is quite unfortunate as she has become very dear to me. I had thought you might be able to grow into a friend, as well, but you have continually proven that wrong. I am uncertain how you have been so blessed with such lovely siblings when you are such a monster. You should utter prayers of thanksgiving every night for their presence in your life. Maybe one day, their sweetness might rub off on you, but I fear that is an empty wish."

Then, without even a nod or any other acknowledgment, Belle turned on her heel, still with Lucy tucked firmly under her arm, and walked away with her maid flapping along in her wake, clucking over her two charges as though she were a hen gathering chicks.

Belle heard Simmons muttering some sort of protest at their departure, but she couldn't be bothered trying to make out what he had said. She was too busy dealing with her own disappointed and shocked feelings. Clearly, she had allowed herself to develop warmer feelings for him than she had even suspected; otherwise, she would not be so devastated in this moment.

Chapter Twenty

Robert watched Isabelle and Lucy hurry away with a maid closely following them who continued to shoot fierce glares towards him over her shoulder even as she remained right on their heels. He felt sick to his stomach. And he rather suspected he might be heartsick, as well.

What a mawkish thought, he reprimanded himself. Viscount Simmons did not get sick to his stomach nor sick in his heart. He turned his back on the image and followed after the men taking Lord Hudson away.

But he couldn't get the image of Lady Isabelle's trembling chin from his mind. The way she had rallied her fierce thoughts and dignity had been a sight to behold. But before she had proven how resilient she was, she had clearly been hurt by his actions. That thought stung far more than it ought to, but he couldn't dwell on it now; he had his investigation to conclude before he dealt with Lady Isabelle and his sister.

The evidence against Lord Hudson was irrefutable, and the bounder well knew it. Before the afternoon had fully seeped into night, the traitor had agreed to accept exile to Botany Bay. It was better than he deserved and well, Hudson knew it. An untitled man would be hung for his offences but their Regent was reluctant to carry out such punishment toward the aristocracy even when they had tried to have him replaced with another ruler.

Robert understood their Sovereign's reluctance, but he didn't agree with it. Any man willing to conspire against the king once was unlikely to cease such stratagems even from the other side of the world. George would not be completely safe as long as Hudson remained alive. But it wasn't Robert's place to offer up his opinion. His role had ended when he had produced the evidence and had the man arrested.

Now he could turn his attention to his own matters. Like what to do with Lucy. Robert knew his brother well enough to be certain Cuthbert wouldn't go away to school until he was convinced Lucy would be comfortable and happy in his absence. The boy didn't trust his own brother enough to leave her in his care. Robert ought to be offended, but instead, he was proud of the cub.

How had their manipulative mother managed to create such sweet children? Robert had only vaguely wondered the matter previously, but now he gave it actual thought. How *had* she done it? Had the children raised themselves? Had it been servants? Or was she perhaps not quite as wicked as he often thought?

As Robert strolled home in the gathering dusk, he allowed his mind to drift back over his past and present, allowing his complicated feelings about conniving women tumble through his thoughts.

When his mother had left him and his father, Robert had been about five years old, he was fairly certain. His mother had often wept before she disappeared, from what he could remember. He had come to the conclusion, as he'd grown older, that she had likely lost a pregnancy, perhaps more than one. Of course, a viscount needed more than one child, in case the worst happened.

Robert had the vaguest memories, from his earliest childhood, of happiness, feelings of contentment, safety, and peace. But all that had been ripped away when his mother had removed herself from his ancestral home. Robert's father had refused to chase after her and bring her back.

Aside from those brief memories of his mother, both the happy and the sad, Robert's other most vivid memories from childhood was of his father ranting about his wife and her scheming ways. Aside from the servants, his father was all Robert had, and he'd loved him with the devotion reserved for a beloved father from his firstborn son. And so Robert had believed every word from his father's lips.

Perhaps she hadn't been as conniving as the old viscount had tried to claim. Perhaps Robert's father had been trying to save face for not having insisted his wife return. Or there were reasons he couldn't fathom. He knew from his own experience that his mother was, in fact, the scheming and conniving sort.

It was true that Lady Simmons, or rather Lady Norton now, had been the usual sort of scheming mother, trying to do all that she could for her children. Perhaps her attempts to coerce him into marriage really were as she claimed, her attempt to do right by Simmons.

But how was he to know?

Robert shook his head. He was a dolt. He could ask the woman.

Norton was nearly a day's ride away. But now that his investigation was concluded, he didn't have much else to do with his time aside from his worries about Lucy and Bert. Perhaps if he had his issues with their mother resolved, he'd be in a better position to solve the dilemma of his brother and sister's future, as well.

To his surprise, Lucy and Bert agreed to accompany him, and they departed early the next morning, surprising their mother by showing up on her doorstep as the afternoon was waning.

He was feeling wrung out from Lucy's chatter and a little worse for the wear of travel, when he was shown into her receiving room.

"Robbie!" Lady Norton exclaimed in a flurry of floating fabric and rose-scented perfume as she hurried to welcome her children to her new home. "And you've brought Lucy and Bert. Are you returning them to me, then?" She appeared to be torn by delight and horror at the thought.

"No, I will be keeping them now, but we thought we ought to call as we haven't seen you in a while."

Lady Norton trilled with laughter. "It hasn't been so long since I've seen the children, but it has been an age since I've seen you. You don't look so well, Robbie. Have you not been sleeping?"

Rather than answer the question, Robert posed one of his own. "I apologise that we've turned up unannounced. Will it be acceptable with your husband if we were to stay overnight?"

Lady Norton frowned at him. "Of course, do stay as long as you'd like. Are you certain you are well?"

"Would it be unbearably rude if I were to leave and visit with the housekeeper?" Lucy interrupted her mother's inquiry while Cuthbert clamoured in with his own wishes. "I'd like to visit in the stables, if it's all the same." Without waiting for a proper response, the youngsters hurried from the room.

Robert's mother shook her head. "You certainly haven't taught them better manners since you've taken them on, have you?"

To his surprise, laughter crowded up his throat, and he chuckled despite his irritation.

"Now sit down and tell me why you've really come all this way. What was so urgent that a letter wouldn't do?"

"Why did Father always say you'd schemed your way into our lives?" He hadn't meant to blurt out his question, but it hadn't been able to keep.

Rather than being dismayed by the question, a gentle smile settled onto Lady Norton's face. "Because the heart is treacherous."

Robert blinked and stared, making his mother sigh.

"Oh, Robbie, you were just so young. You couldn't have understood it. I never should have left, but I couldn't bear to lose any more babies. Did you know we lost three?"

"I always wondered if that was why you had left. But what does that have to do with schemes?"

"That wasn't the schemes your father was referring to. He never wanted to love me, if you must know. He resented loving me. And he hated that our love turned sour when I lost the children. So I did have to trick him to finally return. I told him I'd fallen in love with someone, and he had to either take me back or suffer the scandal. He wouldn't believe that I'd had a change of heart. But all pain dulls with time, even the tragedy of losing the bairns. It doesn't go away, mind you, but it isn't so sharp. And so I was able to realise that it was you I was missing out on with my foolishness. Your father had gotten used to my being gone, though, I suppose, and just as he hadn't wanted to love me in the first place, he was all the more determined not to allow me to return. So I enlisted the help of the servants. I turned up in his bed, to his surprise, and he didn't turn me away after that. And soon your sister came along. We never lost another babe after that. But it wasn't many years before we lost your father."

"And so I was left with the impression that you had tricked your way back into our lives."

"Which wasn't untrue," his mother answered with a gentle smile.

"But it was for the best, then, wasn't it?"

"I would like to think so," Lady Norton answered with her smile widening into a grin. "But I know my way of doing things, coupled with your father's expressions, created in you a certain view of things and a dreadfully suspicious attitude."

"Ought I to apologise, then?"

Lady Norton shrugged. "Not necessarily. You came by your feelings honestly. It was poorly done of me to leave you for so many of your most formative years. And despite my deep love for my children, I was never the most demonstrative mother. Just as your father had never wanted to love me, I didn't want to love my children, so deep was my fear of losing them." The woman sighed. "Feelings can be really stupid sometimes."

Robert had to laugh and agree. He then proceeded to pour out all his concerns to his mother, starting with his worries about Lucy, and then telling him about Lady Bathurst's schemes to pair him up with her daughter.

"Oh Robbie. Your sister has always been a mystery to me. I do thank you for taking the pair of them off my hands. They are lovely children, but you will do better with them than I have done. Norton wasn't expecting them to remain with us permanently, but right at first, I insisted I needed to have them, but you were right to take them, now that I've married. I should have realised sooner."

"Do you think to have more children?" He was rather aghast at the thought but he was uncertain if it might even be possible for her.

His mother's laughter filled the room. "No. Norton is satisfied with the children he already has; he merely wanted my company, if you can believe it."

"Company might be nice," Robert added.

"I've been trying to convince you to wed for years now, but don't do it for Lucy's sake, Robert. I want you to find happiness and love. Don't resist it as your father always did." She paused for a moment and studied his face. "Lady Bathurst most likely wasn't truly trying to compromise her daughter. You didn't say she ever connived to have the two of you found alone, did she?"

"No," Robert denied hotly. "I would never participate in such a disaster."

"That is not the point I'm making, my son. I am saying that you have always had a shrouded inclination toward any woman you think might be entertaining stratagems. A mother is forced to employ them at times. You have to accept that and believe that doesn't make her wicked. I agree with you that it would have been wicked if the woman was actually trying to ruin her daughter's reputation in order to force you into a marriage with her. But isn't it possible they were merely trying to throw the two of you together and just went about it in the most awkward fashion, much as I had to do with your father?"

Robert stared at his mother in consternation. Explained like that, he had to admit he had been unforgivably rude to Lady Isabelle. And she had been nothing but kindness to his sister. His heartbeat roared in his ears. Would she ever be able to forgive him?

"We have to return to London." He stood to take his leave.

"Don't be daft, my son. You would ruin your horses on these horrible roads in the dark of night. Stay at least the night. If the girl will have you, it will keep another day at this point."

Robert swallowed his frustration and accepted the wisdom of his mother's words.

Chapter Twenty-One

Belle still hadn't recovered from her last encounter with Viscount Simmons. She ought to be strolling on Bond Street or visiting Lady Chloe or some other means of encountering eligible gentlemen. But after she had stood and watched Lord Hudson being arrested, the first man she had thought might be an acceptable potential husband, all confidence in her own judgement had evaporated, and a sense of despair threatened to swamp her. She refused to think it might have anything to do with Lord Simmons' determination to despise her.

Lord Simmons' feelings meant nothing to her. Perhaps if she told herself that often enough she might even begin to believe it. Except, she kept remembering the odd tingles she'd experience whenever they'd be near each other. Well, perhaps not that last time when he had berated her for bringing his sister to the park where he was arresting a man.

But what were they doing conducting their investigation where decent people could be found?

That was what she wanted to know even as she denied to herself that she was being consumed with curiosity about the investigation and how Robert was involved, and what had he been thinking?—aside from his negative thoughts about her—he hadn't left her in any doubt about those.

With another sigh that felt as though it had come from the depths of her soul, Belle paced the small salon. She ought to be out, engaged in her campaign of finding herself a new home, but no matter where she looked, she couldn't get her heart into the spirit of the matter, and it just wasn't going to happen for her that day, nor even that week. She would have her maid tell her mother she had a megrim. All Belle wanted to do was take to her bed. That sounded appallingly dramatic and melancholy even to her own ears, but Belle couldn't find in herself to care that day. She would do so tomorrow, she promised herself as she moved toward the door.

In her befuddled state, her pace was so slow that it wasn't the quick affair it should have been. Thus, she was still in the room when she heard a commotion at the front of the house. Was she beginning to imagine things? That couldn't possibly be Robert's voice! She tiptoed out into the hallway to peer over the railing and could barely believe the sight before her.

It was Robert Scranton, Viscount Simmons. She nearly fell over the banister in her shock, but she managed not to make a squeak. She scurried back into the salon, suddenly no longer interested in returning to bed.

Why was he here? What did he want? He surely hadn't come to berate her anew, had he?

Belle resumed her pacing, but this time, it was much more rigorous as her feet tried to keep pace with her racing thoughts.

The door opened, and the butler announced, "Lord Simmons to see you, my lady."

Belle turned toward the door in shock as her one hand reached toward her hair and the other wanted to clutch her throat with surprise. She ought to have taken the opportunity to return to her room after all. She was not dressed for gentleman visitors.

But she had never allowed herself to be so missish in all her days; she wasn't about to start that day. Belle forced her arms to relax as she straightened to her full height, lifting her chin to meet her visitor's gaze.

"Good afternoon, Lord Simmons, I'm surprised to meet you here."

Despite her cool reception, a warm smile spread across the man's handsome face, and Belle's knees threatened to weaken on her. She gestured a little vaguely toward a chair and took a seat on one herself.

"To what do I owe this pleasure?" she tried to keep the backbone in her voice, at least, even if her actual bones had turned soft on her.

Her manner didn't seem to dampen the gentleman's warmth toward her, much to her surprise. He did take a seat, but it was not the one she had indicated. To Belle's shock and dismay, he sat himself as near to her as could be managed without removing her to the settee, and he somehow managed to possess himself of her hand.

Of course, Belle didn't object, but she attributed that to her lingering shock over his presence.

"Are you well?" he finally asked, his searching gaze seeming to devour her features.

"Of course," she replied, softer than she'd intended. "Why wouldn't I be?" she asked, rallying.

"My sister has explained to me that in my surprise over the two of you finding yourselves in the vicinity of my operation, I might have been far harsher than I intended."

Heat filled her cheeks, but Belle didn't allow herself to soften any further. "I cannot comment on how harsh you intended to be, but I will agree with Miss Lucy that you were very angry toward me. I suppose, considering you were involved in some sort of operation, as you say, you considered yourself entitled to your reaction, but how could we have possibly known you had occupied that park? We were surely not the only innocent people with whom you crossed paths."

"You are quite correct, therefore, my apology."

Under other circumstances, Belle might have laughed over his turn of the phrase and his tone. But even his contrite expression didn't really appease her. He had hurt her feelings. It might be an overreaction on her part, but she couldn't help it. Despite her efforts to keep her focus on finding a husband that was *not* Viscount Simmons, somehow the man had made his way into her feelings in a warmer way than she should have allowed.

But that was her problem, not his fault. Taking a deep breath, Belle made an effort to curb her hurt and be gracious.

"Is that why you've come, my lord? To absolve yourself of guilt? Or were you perhaps going to offer to share some information with me? I might withhold my forgiveness on the condition that you satisfy my curiosity."

To her surprise, he laughed. It was genuine laughter, rich and deep, and it caused tingles to flutter anew in Belle's midsection, a sensation she found very difficult to ignore as heat climbed back into her cheeks. He must have mistaken her blush, thankfully, as he apologised again.

"I wasn't having fun at your expense, my lady," he began stiffly. "I was amused by your attempt at blackmail."

Belle's blush deepened if that were even possible.

"Very well, I will tell you what I can, but it must be kept in confidence."

Belle lifted her eyebrows as haughtily as she could muster. "You would entrust me with confidences, my lord? Surely you jest."

He had the grace to blush over her ribbing, but she hastily offered an apology. "That was ill-mannered of me, my lord," she said with a wave of her hand. "Please tell me what you can. I can keep a secret, but I understand if you must do so, as well."

"Thank you, my lady. You have been all that is kind to my sister. and I have rewarded you with hard feelings at every turn. I cannot blame you for being cross with me."

"Lucy is a delight and remarkably easy to be kind towards, but I thank you if your words mean you shan't be restricting her company from mine in the future."

"That is, in fact, what I wished to talk to you about, my lady," Robert told her hesitantly, causing Belle to frown in confusion. "Your future company," he added, in an attempt at explanation.

"You'd like advice about Lucy? Is that why you've called, then?" Belle was puzzled. The previous time he had asked her about something pertaining to his sister, she hadn't been of much help.

"No," Robert said with a huff in his voice. "I'm making a mull of this. I seem to make a mull of everything when it comes to you. I do apologise." He took a deep breath and then reached out to clasp one of her hands. "My dear lady, I know you are in search of a husband. And I find myself in need of a wife. I was wondering, if you would be so kind, if you might consider me for the position."

Belle blinked and stared, shifting her gaze between their clasped hands and the viscount's face, a frown creasing her forehead.

"You think to wed with me?" she asked, dazed by the thought but inclined to reject his offer instinctively despite the warm feelings she had developed toward him, very much against her will. "But you don't think well of me. That surely wouldn't lend itself to a successful pairing, would it, my lord?"

Robert sighed. "I very much do think well of you, my lady," he insisted. "I'm still not doing this correctly. I am afraid I was prejudiced against you because of your parents' manipulations. My mother is like that, and I have been quite opposed to such behaviour. I read worse intentions into your parents' actions than perhaps were warranted, and it led me to judge you harshly, so I rejected my attraction to you for the past few weeks. But someone helped me realise that perhaps I have been wrong in my assessment. And that led me to accept the feelings that have been growing within me. Toward you, that is," he added with a nervous laugh that contrarily put Belle much more at ease.

"You have developed feelings for me and think we ought to wed?" Belle repeated slowly, still trying to decide how she felt about this sudden change of circumstances.

"Did I really sound so pitifully bloodless as I said it, my dear?" Robert asked with another laugh, this one sounding a little less awkward than the last. Suddenly, he stood up and pulled her up with him. Before she could even blink, he had pulled her into his arms and his head was descending towards hers.

His lips settled over her own, and Belle found all thought had fled. It didn't last long, but when he lifted his head from hers, he no longer appeared uncertain, but that was the only thought that would form in Belle's befuddled mind.

"My lady Isabelle, I have, much to my surprised delight, fallen quite deeply in love with you. I am sorry that I resisted the sensation so fiercely, but it seems to be quite a persistent emotion. Please say you will do me the great honor of being my wife."

Belle blinked as her muddled thoughts and feelings of the past few weeks realigned themselves in her mind and heart. Suddenly, all the denials of the emotions she had toward the viscount as a sort of self-preservation against his apparent rejection of her were no longer needed, and all the love for him that had grown, filled her being. A grin split her face. "Well, why didn't you say that from the beginning?" she asked with a laugh. "That was all I needed to hear."

Before she could say anything more, he shouted with laughter and then effectively silenced any possible recriminations by sealing their lips with another kiss.

Epilogue

Isabelle sat in the window seat watching her family through the glass. It was getting more difficult to curl in the space with her growing belly, but it was still one of her favourite spots in the entire large house she shared with her husband, his young siblings, and their own growing family. Her hand curved over her protrusion once more. If her calculations were correct, the timing was going to be perfect. This much-anticipated darling would be safely arrived and settled in time for her to escort Lucy for her debut.

How had the time flown so? Belle supposed it was the joy that filled their house that did that trick. It had been thusly since the day Lord Simmons had hurried her to an altar to wed her. As soon as he had made up his mind to love her, he hadn't allowed time to pass lest she change her mind.

She would never do so. Robert Scranton, Viscount Simmons, was more than perfect for her. And his viscountess had cherished taking his sister in hand before they'd started their own family. Even though it had concerned Isabelle how long it had taken for their first child to arrive on the scene, wondering if there was some problem with her childbearing ability, in hindsight, the delay had been good for the rest of the family.

Cuthbert had been comfortable leaving his sister in their capable hands as he'd happily gone off to Eton the autumn after they'd wed, and Lucy had even become a day student at a pleasant school near Simmons. Not for long, mind you, as she never wanted to be separated from her new sister, but Lucy had blossomed into the beautiful young woman Isabelle had always known she would be.

Belle hoped this babe would be a girl. Robert already had his heir. His beloved heir that was surely having his appetite spoiled as he nibbled on the sweets both his father and his aunt were sharing with him while she watched. Both seemed to think they were keeping it hidden, but nothing was hidden from a mother's eyes.

Isabelle glanced down at the letter in her hand. Her friend Amelia, Lady Everleigh now that Lord Adelaide had inherited his father's earldom, was already making plans to host another one of her house parties and thought Belle should bring Lucy. Amelia had turned into the worst, or perhaps the best matchmaker and thought Lucy might be a match for her youngest brother-in-law.

Belle was hesitant. She had no desire to hurry Lucy into marriage. They had already held her home a year longer than many of her peers with the thought that she ought not to be rushed into a commitment. But they had all finally agreed for her to make her debut once Belle was safely delivered of this baby. Still, there was no need to conspire about a match with the most successful matchmaker of her acquaintance.

In a few years, if necessary, she would consider it. In the meantime, Belle thought, her family was waiting for her. It was time for her to cease watching and rejoin them.

Her heart was full as she hurried to follow her actions to her thoughts, and her husband's ready arms closed around her even as she lifted her son over her bump and smiled at her beloved Lucy.

The End

Read the next book in the *Northcott Kinship* series:

Defying the Earl

Lord Braxton has just inherited an earldom. His mixed feelings on the subject are a distraction from his duties to the Home Office. Further distracting him is the bet his friends have made that he cannot get the beautiful but frosty Lady Beatrice to be more friendly. This opposites-attract, enemies to love, stuck together romance is sure to melt your heart.

After that, follow Lucy Scranton's adventures, the final book in the *Northcott Kinship* series:

Confounding the Fortune Hunter

The *Northcott Kinship* series is connected to the *Sherton Sisters*. Have you read those yet?

Start with Book 1:

A Duke to Elude

She's waiting for true love. He's tasked with uncovering the truth. When nefarious schemes threaten her reputation, he finds his heart on the line with it.

About the Author

I learned to read when I was four or five, listening to my mother read to me when I was lonely after my brother started school. Ever since, I've had my head buried in books. I love words – historical plaques, signs, the cereal box – but my first love has always been novels.

A little over ten years ago my husband dared me to write a book instead of always reading them. I didn't think I'd be able to do it, but to my surprise I love writing. Those early efforts eventually became my first published book – *Tempting the Earl* (published by Avalon Books in 2010). It has been a thrilling adventure as I learned to navigate the world of publishing.

I believe firmly that everyone deserves a happily ever after. I want my readers to be able to escape from the everyday for a little while and feel upbeat and refreshed when they get to the end of my books.

When not reading or writing, I can be found traipsing around my neighbourhood or travelling the world with my favourite companion.

Stay in touch:

Website Facebook Instagram TikTok

Stay in touch with Wendy May Andrews
and all her upcoming publishing news.

Sign up for her biweekly newsletter

Other books by Wendy May Andrews

Collect all books in this series:

Northcott Kinship

Intriguing Lord Adelaide

Convincing Mr. Northcott

Evading the Gentleman

Distracting the Heir

Provoking Lord Simmons

Defying the Earl

Confounding the Fortune Hunter

Another breathtaking series you don't want to miss:

The Ladies of Mayfair - Book 1:

The Governess' Debut

The governess must charm both the spoiled child and the haughty earl.

Orphaned and destitute, gently born Felicia Scott must find a way to keep a roof over her head. No longer able to enter the Marriage Mart, but also not of the servant class, the only option is to find a position as governess.

After his spoiled, seven year old daughter has sent off three governesses in the 18 months since her mother died, the Earl of Standish doubts the young, inexperienced Miss Scott could possible manage the position. Since he's desperate and she comes so highly recommended, the earl agrees to give her a chance. Much to everyone's amazement, the beautiful, young governess succeeds where the others had failed. The entire household benefits from the calm, including the jaded earl.

How does he overcome his arrogance to see his governess' true value?

Available now on Amazon

If you like Regencies with a touch of adventure, you will love the *Mayfair Mayhem* series.

Book 1 is:

The Duke Conspiracy

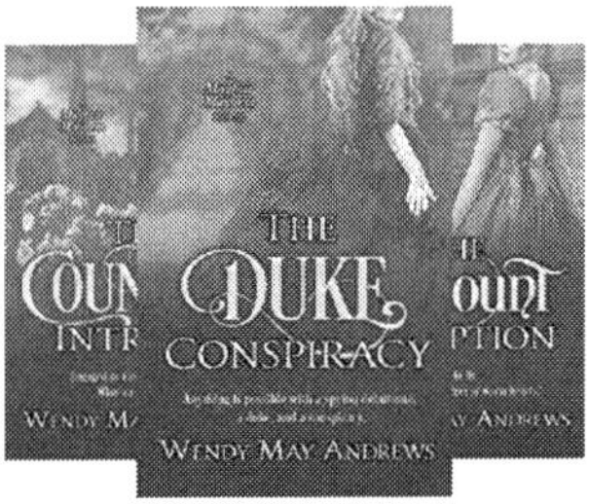

Anything is possible with a spying debutante, a duke, and a conspiracy.

Growing up, Rose and Alex were the best of friends until their families became embroiled in a feud. Now, the Season is throwing them into each other's company. Despite the spark of attraction they might feel for one another, they each want very different things in life, besides needing to support their own family's side in the dispute.

Miss Rosamund Smythe is finding the Season to be a dead bore after spying with her father, a baron diplomat, in Vienna. She wants more out of life than just being some nobleman's wife. When she overhears a plot to entrap Alex into a marriage of convenience, her intrigue and some last vestige of loyalty causes them to overcome the feud.

His Grace, Alexander Milton, the Duke of Wrentham, wants a quiet life with a "proper" wife after his tumultuous childhood. His parents had fought viciously, lied often, and Alex had hated it all.

Rose's meddling puts her in danger. Alex will have to leave the simple peace he craves to claim a love he never could have imagined. Can they claim their happily ever after despite the turmoil?

Available now on Amazon

Like Regency Romance?

Read Book 1 in the *Bequest Series*

Inheriting Trouble

The inheritance was meant to better her life, not muddle it.

Georgia Holton, wellborn but nearly penniless, is best friends with one of the Earl of Sherton's five daughters. When she is invited to accompany her friend for two weeks of the Season, Georgia jumps at the opportunity to have a little adventure away from her small village.

The Earl of Crossley is handsome, wealthy, widowed, and jaded. He has no intention of courting any of this Season's debutantes. After all, every woman he's ever known has been dishonest, including his late wife. But when a chance encounter throws him into contact with the Sherton ladies and their lovely friend, he can't help being drawn to Georgia's beauty and endearing personality.

When confusion about Georgia's small inheritance becomes known, a sense of obligation to right a wrong, forces the earl and Georgia into close association.

But is she really different from any of the other women, or does she have an ulterior motive?

And can Georgia even consider getting close to a man from High Society, when all she wants is to return to her simple village life?

Sparks fly between these two, but it will take forgiveness and understanding on both their parts to reach a happily ever after.

Available now on Amazon

You don't want to miss the series connected to *The Northcott Kinship* you've just read:

The Sherton Sisters - Book 1:

A Duke to Elude

She's waiting for true love. He's tasked with uncovering the truth. When nefarious schemes threaten her reputation, he finds his heart on the line with it.

Lady Rosabel, eldest daughter of the Earl of Sherton, has no interest in being a Duchess, despite countless proposals from eligible nobility. Secretly, she is waiting for a love match—preferably with someone who carries no title. Bel's third Season is predictably disappointing until the mysterious Duke of Wexford arrives and has her questioning her plans to refuse any suitor with his status.

James Allingham, the 6th Duke of Wexford, seems to have inherited the role as advisor to the ailing King along with the dukedom. Investigating Lord Prescott's schemes is tricky enough without the interference of Lady Rosabel. She is beautiful and intelligent, but Wexford has no time for courting.

Wexford needs to uncover everything about Prescott's plans to destabilize the colonies. When Lady Rosabel is implicated in the schemes, James fights his suspicions of—and his attraction to—the beautiful young woman as he presses on to find the truth.

Discover the page-turning intrigue of this clean Regency romance today!

Available now on Amazon

Printed in Dunstable, United Kingdom

71048947R00138